THE PARACHUTE

The PARACHUTE

SINCLAIR DUMONTAIS

translated by PATRICIA CLAXTON

KEY PORTER BOOKS

Éditions Hurtubise HMH
1815, avenue De Lorimier
Montréal, QC H2K 3W6
Canada

Library and Archives Canada Cataloguing in Publication

Dumontais, Sinclair
[Parachute de Socrate. English]
    The parachute : a sadly funny novel about the consumption of consumers / Sinclair
Dumontais ; translated by Patricia Claxton.

Translation of: Le parachute de Socrate.
ISBN 1-55263-734-4

    I. Claxton, Patricia, 1929– II. Title. III. Title: Parachute de Socrate. English.

PS8607.U46P3713 2005   C843'.6   C2005-902460-7

The publisher gratefully acknowledges the support of the Canada Council for the Arts
and the Ontario Arts Council for its publishing program. We acknowledge the support
of the Government of Ontario through the Ontario Media Development Corporation's
Ontario Book Initiative.

We acknowledge the financial support of the Government of Canada through the Book
Publishing Industry Development Program (BPIDP) for our publishing activities.

Key Porter Books Limited
Six Adelaide Street East, Tenth Floor
Toronto, Ontario
Canada M5C 1H6

www.keyporter.com

Text design: Ingrid Paulson
Electronic formatting: Beth Crane, Heidy Lawrance Associates

Printed and bound in Canada

05 06 07 08 09 5 4 3 2 1

I dedicate this book to the hard-working children
who, thanks to us — myself included —
will never be able to read it

WHERE did you say? There, at the end of the table? Of course, of course. I've come to talk, not listen, so that's the place for me. I'll go there right now. Ah, Madam, are you also attending the meeting? I see. I'd rather it be strictly men, but never mind.

There. No, thank you. I don't need anything. Or rather, yes. A large glass of water. Very cold. I'll be doing a lot of talking, and what I have to say will flow better. I'd advise you to take one yourself. It's good for one's thoughts. I doubt you have any, but you might be a bit more alert. That will be for the better, at least.

Ah, Mr. President, nice to see you again. I'm ready, yes. I've been waiting for a glass of water for a quarter of an hour, but we can start anyway. Yes, yes. I agree. Entirely. Neither you nor I have any time to waste. I'll let you take your place, then I'll begin. Your sheep are already in their seats.

Let's begin without further ado.

So, Mr. President, Lady and Gentlemen of the Board of Directors, good morning. I will not introduce myself because you all know who I am.

Three months ago to the day, Mr. President, you asked me to take a look at your company and present what would appropriately be called an action plan for the coming years.

Not that your company is sick. You have been writing the rule book for over twenty years in an industry that has become one of the most lucrative there are, in all countries where men and women are also consumers. Your sales are steady while your production costs are falling. You operate in precisely sixty-two countries. You are achieving record margins everywhere, which is making your shareholders rich, and also your accountants, your lawyers, your brokers, your bankers, and of course yourselves and your loved ones. Your grandchildren are going to be far richer than I am now.

Your liquidities have enabled you to buy out an appreciable number of your competitors, then of your suppliers, and sometimes even ministers who have qualms about fixing laws to suit your purpose.

Your company is the very picture of success. Not a week goes by without its achievements being mentioned in economic publications or studied in American or

European universities. In certain circles, you, Mr. President, are a star. Which you cultivate admirably, I might say, by hardly ever giving interviews, keeping company with a few movie stars, and very skilfully managing the circulation of a rumour or two from time to time.

Despite your company's exceptional performance, you're worried, and that is why you have asked me with such urgency to leave my semi-retirement and attend to your future. You're afraid of running out of steam. You feel it imperative to prepare an offensive that will guarantee your empire continued growth for many tomorrows. You sense danger around the corner. A threat. An enemy lurking in the shadows. You don't know why, you don't know how, you don't know when, but you know the day will come when you will reach a ceiling which, even if it merely remains static, will in effect be a kind of decline because your shareholders will never allow you simply to earn them dividends. They'll want those benefits multiplied over and over again.

Their greed is the engine of our century.

You're right, furthermore. I mean, you're right to be afraid. Your instinct has not failed you. Unless you get moving at once, your company will very soon reach the point of no return beyond which it will begin to decline, or even get eaten up. By whom, you may ask, since none of your competitors are big enough to hurt you? By none other than itself, of course. Like a bear that eats its own fat while it sleeps.

Fortunately, you were not asleep. The proof is that you called me, Mr. President. You said, "My dear friend, I have a commission of the utmost importance for you."

And I replied, "Yes, indeed. Of the utmost importance. Call a meeting of your Board in precisely three months, and be prepared to make the most spectacular change of direction ever made by a company in the entire modern age."

That is why I'm here before you today.

If you had given me this commission ten years ago when I was reaching the peak of my career (as you are in your own field today), a career of international scope, as you know, if you had sought my advice during the period when I was in constant demand, giving dozens of speeches monthly to chambers of commerce, professional associations, governments, and exclusive clubs, and advising the most influential men on the planet, I would have wasted no time mobilizing a powerful machine capable of gathering and synthesizing all existing data on your product, your market, and its outlook. I'd have sent expert survey teams out into the field, I'd have gathered groups of consumers so as to read their gut reactions, I'd have paid agents to infiltrate the competition, I'd have asked people of all ages and walks of life to go into the streets and talk to others and then come and tell me what really goes on in people's lives. I would have lunched with sociologists, psychologists, anthropologists, and economists, and I'd have asked five different teams— yes, five–to develop projections for the future, without consulting among them, and then put each team through a merciless grilling, and out of all this would have emerged the strategy you expect from me.

In this, I have always been the undisputed master. Everyone knew that working for me would prove a man's worth, even if it would also guarantee to put him through several months of hell, because I would drain every one of those men. I would drain them of everything their minds and bodies could bear. For the benefit of my clients, of course, but also for my own prestige because my methods are considered unbeatable.

Lady and Gentlemen, this time I have done none of those things. The very next day after accepting this commission, I took a plane for Greece.

I returned only this morning. And don't be surprised that I came back empty-handed. The only document I'll submit to you today will be my bill. The things I'm going to tell you are so seriously confidential that I have not risked carrying them anywhere but in my head. When I leave this room, I shall have delivered to you orally my Olympian reflection and, in detail, the strategy to be followed so that in years to come, Mr. President, you will be the undisputed celebrity of a century that will be called yours.

I shall insist that none of you write anything during this peroration so that you can concentrate on understanding what I'm talking about, which will be indispensable.

I mean you too, Madam. Put down your pencil, please. And unplug your computer so that no one could imagine that you might be transmitting my knowledge in real time to those hordes in the business of business espionage. A person in your position, Madam, has to know something about suspicion management.

Thank you.

In Greece, I lived on one of those islands that remember nothing but Antiquity. Surrounded by those old stones that do not know what a hamburger is, or a motorcycle, or a cellular telephone, I shut myself away from the world and set about an icy analysis of what civilization has become and what it will be tomorrow. I put aside the method of work I myself developed over the course of my career, the one that has won me so much admiration and also so many enemies, and at the top of a hill, looking down at the Mediterranean, I sat and thought. I thought for the three months I asked you to give me, alone with our past already traced and our future to be faced.

I have not done any research on your product, your market, or your competitors. I have not ordered any surveys. I have not spoken to any specialists. I have given no instructions to nor bled dry any of the ambitious young bucks who are jostling to succeed me. After my years of experience, I have to say, this investigation has not taught me much I did not know already. Societies are the mirror of man: they evolve very slowly and always predictably. A curve tracing the last two or three centuries will serve to plot a sufficiently precise projection for the next ten years. And then, this time I have no desire to move heaven and earth. To tell the truth, it's not fun any more.

You're worried, aren't you? You're already wondering whether you're going to end up throwing my bill in my face. Whether I've let you down. Perhaps you're even waiting for me to take a mouthful of water so you can interrupt what I'm saying and show me the door.

That would be a mistake. It would also indicate you were overlooking what I told you the day I accepted this commission, Mr. President. Do you remember? I told you that this would be the last of my career, a career that I was determined to end spectacularly. I have a reputation for being proud, arrogant, and most of all a winner. I therefore owe you the most brilliant analysis and recommendation of my career, and I shall deliver.

That said, I shall now take a mouthful of water. In all tranquility and at the risk of irritating you. I do have a flair for drama, don't I? My grandfather was an actor. I have to show respect for the art that was his passion. Forgive me for seeming so imperious; it's a privilege I allow myself. I'm not just anyone, after all. I'm the one you've called on to soothe your anxieties.

Now.

What's so marvellous about these islands is that they immerse us in a very distant past without cutting us off from civilization. They are separated from the world not by space, but by time.

If I'd decided to withdraw to some unknown, over-looked area, one of those rare spots yet to interest man, I would have found myself in a time before any civilization. In a world without man, yes, but also without history. In Greece, on that island I chose for being tiny, sparsely populated, and recorded on maps for centuries, I was still in civilization, still part of it, but it had remained a civilization previous to ours.

The difference is vital, believe me. Do you like walking in the woods? As long as all you come across are trees, you can let your imagination make you believe you're the very first human to set foot in that place. You're both an explorer and a settler. You're alone on Earth, and you can belong in any century because you've seen no trace of history. But from the moment you trip over a stone, and you discover that that stone is lined up with other stones, and there are vestiges of a foundation there, however little you think of yourself as a man and the son of many generations, a kind of nostalgia takes hold of you. You relive in imagination that time long ago when an ancestor toiled a whole day cutting the wood that would become the roof under which many households of descendants would be born. You're no longer a settler; you're now an archaeologist, an historian, a witness to evolution.

The Greek island I'm telling you about is full of these old stones said to be historical. Since no one has seen advantage in modernizing them, I spent my time in the past, in a manner of speaking, amid ruins dating back several thousand years. So the land I was on was just the way it was before men were aware that the Earth is round. An age, I'd even say, before the invention of man– I mean man as we know him today, who is modern, accomplished, and first and foremost a consumer.

Lady and Gentlemen, for three months I observed the wide world of today with the eye of the tiny world of yesterday. Sitting among those ruins, overlooking the most beautiful sea in the world, I saw the film of history over again. I saw pass before my mind's eye all that led as slowly as a slug to the motorcycle, the hamburger, and the cellular telephone.

I confess that this journey in time upset me considerably. And this old man I am today, whose degrees, reputation, and accomplishments are envied by everyone, this old man suffered what you would call a shock.

Not the kind of shock you might think, mind you. No, I was not sucked in by all those curiously popular fabulations that would have some believe that we have fatally vandalized the Earth and must with all haste return to a preindustrial mentality. I have never worked with anything but progress in view, and it would take a lot to convince me that History needs remaking. On the contrary, I adhere wholeheartedly to the theory that holds that nothing is created or destroyed. Which means that all we have supposedly destroyed still exists today, but simply in another form. Nothing has left our atmosphere; everything is still beneath the screen that separates us from the cosmos. People who keep trying to denounce what we have done lash out at Darwin and all the theories of evolution, which puts them in flagrant contradiction with their own principles.

What has struck me, you see, is the lack of ambition on the part of our corporations. You have brought me here today on an urgent mission because you feel that your activities are going to flatten out. Meanwhile, there are societies in which people are still peasants and can't even be called consumers because we don't sell them anything.

Or hardly anything. What sloppiness, don't you think? Today we've come to the point of selling our own citizens fifth, even tenth-generation products and services, meaning totally useless stuff, while we don't get around to turning people who are still peasants into consumers. And Lord knows there are plenty of them. Greece isn't Africa!

Decidedly, there are still gaps in the curricula of the major schools of administration and management. They neglect the teaching of geography.

This said, I have not come down from this precommercial mount to preach to you. On the contrary. Shortly I shall be proposing a more Machiavellian plan to you than anything you could imagine. I just want to say this: if I had not chosen this period of isolation, I would have presented the same plan without knowing it was Machiavellian. Today I know, which allows me to concoct it more adroitly, more confidently, more boldly too. With the claws of a lion that's not moved one iota by the gazelle's laments.

And allows me above all, yes, above all, to package it without scruples. How can you pursue your growth with your feet tangled in the ropes of self-respect? Today, scruples are the only ramparts still raised against so-called abuse.

Why without scruples? Because I'm sixty-seven years old, Mr. President. I have no family and no heirs. My mother gave birth three times, and I am her youngest child. She did not survive my birth, and my father died over ten years ago. My wife left me the day her husband became a career, and we had no children. I have two nephews and a niece I do not know. So what does it matter what I leave behind? In a few years, I too will be only a stone. A tombstone, to be precise. Whether people lay flowers on it or spit on it in disgust will make no difference to my rest. A well-deserved rest, too.

You're paying me to learn what your company should do in order to keep growing. I shall tell you dispassionately, simply, and without scruples. My contribution to evolution will have been complete and faithful up to the last minute of my existence.

I could have turned down this contract, of course. I have earned enough money to date to be able to live my final years in comfort and luxury. Especially since I've never been able to spend all the wealth that's been showered on me. Money is like jam. Only being deprived of it makes you want it. I'm worth a substantial sum then, that's nicely protected, and nothing obliges me to offer you my services.

If I accepted this contract, Lady and Gentlemen, it wasn't for money or some other favour. It was because I knew, because I had decided, that it would be my last. And without a future, this being the last day of my life in a manner of speaking, I would have total freedom. Freedom to formulate a free strategy. Yes, free. Unfair, indeed, but totally free. You know as well as I do that we have to choose between fairness and freedom, and if it's true in life, it's even more true in business.

The money we get has to be got from someone.

So here is a strategy that is free of any hesitation, free of any respect, free of any likely remorse. An unfair strategy, meaning designed to win, without concern for anyone or anything and still less for future generations, since its premise is that there is no need for me to be concerned.

Your eyes are shining, I see, Mr. President. Could it be you're already sold on my strategies before even hearing them? I'd bet on it. I'm flattered by your confidence in me. You're showing me proof that I've lost none of my verve.

Before getting down to the crux of the matter, allow me one last comment on that Greek island which I left yesterday morning and to which I shall return the instant I have received my fee. While I do not need the money, I am determined to cash this cheque because its endorsement will be the signature that shows I consider my life's work to be finished.

What I want to point out to you, Mr. President, is that the island on which I was staying is a piece of land surrounded by water. You'll tell me that's obvious, and it's true. You're a man who travels often to the world's great cities. Do you know that Manhattan, the very centre of New York, is an island? New Yorkers don't know it. Why? I'll tell you. Because Manhattan ceased to be an island a long time ago. An island, Mr. President, is a place cut off from the world. With Manhattan, the opposite is the case—it's everywhere else that's cut off from the world. I would not be surprised in fact if the individuals who guide our fortunes from the summit of this new Olympus were possessed of the innocent certainty that the rest of the continent is an island. The proof being that one always has to cross a bridge to reach it.

Furthermore, if the city has developed vertically, don't think it's owing to lack of space. Essentially, it's the need to taste the headiness of heights. Isn't it exciting to reach the top of the world in a few seconds, straight up in an elevator, when others will take a lifetime and a thousand detours to mount a single step? What bliss…

Now I shall not bore you further with my observations. Before you begin to think I've turned into a tour guide, I shall deliver the considered opinion you have commissioned from me and for which you are going to pay me so handsomely.

Oh, one last thing before I begin, Mr. President. Are you quite sure of the usefulness of all these people here today? I don't mean their usefulness to the company. That's for them to justify. I mean their usefulness at this meeting. It seems to me there are a lot of ears present for very little grey matter.

Well. As you wish. But I want to say that in no case can I be held responsible for possible leaks. People I've known have made very long careers with two or three ideas plucked out of my head. Like musicians who build whole lives on two guitar chords.

———•———

WE shall begin, if you will allow, with a very brief and very down-to-earth analysis of the situation. Your situation, of course.

You manufacture shoes. To all appearances, at least. I shall not go into the history of these items for which people spend veritable fortunes today. It will suffice for us to recall that shoes began as simple foot coverings. To enable us to walk in summer without hurting our feet and in winter without freezing them.

Today, footwear has a place in the codes of the various strata of our society. It has become one of the credentials that opens doors in the right places. By bringing it into the world of esthetics, we have given it a social value, which allows you not just to live off it, but to profit from it enormously. This is what your company considers "capital appreciation," and is "appreciation of value" to your customers.

You have known for a very long time that this industry's profitability lies less in sales of shoes than in sales of the brand names you place on them. The design of shoes, initially concerned with making them comfortable, has become less important than the design of their brands. We're talking here of their names, logos, packaging, in-store presentation, and even traditions created around them. These brands are vastly more profitable at the cash registers than the shoes that carry them, in a manner of speaking. You get this imaginary value, which you have created out of thin air, into our heads and onto our feet, and it lets you sell your pumps and chukkas at ten to thirty times their factory cost. We're not buying the shoe, we're buying the name stamped on it and the prestige it gives us to wear it.

What is more, what you've been selling for a number of years now is not so much the brands you've created as your reputation as the manufacturer of these brands. The design of your brands has lost importance to the design of your reputation. Building a reputation is very expensive, of course, but the result is undoubtedly prof-itable and its useful life, providing it's well managed, is extraordinarily long. So you have built, and sold, your reputation. Your real customers are no longer the buyers of shoes but the shareholders of this reputation, whose value is measured on the stock exchange. The profit you take is directly linked to the fact that this reputation has no leather, no seams, and no pay. Your gain is phenomenal.

Once you understood that reputations are fixed in the minds of individuals, you followed reputation design with the design of individuals. So today you manufacture shoes, of course, and brands and a reputation, but you also and above all manufacture individuals. In a way, you manufacture your customers, and those customers indirectly guarantee that your stock market value will increase. This increase is a direct function of your ability to educate those customers the way parents educate their children: this is good, that's bad, take care not to burn yourself, don't follow strangers, look both ways before crossing the street, be polite, wash your hands before coming to the table, etc. Except that you're terrifically "cool" parents because your exhortations aren't restrictions. They're the opposite. They're freedoms, permissions, and encouragements: have fun with your friends, laugh and be merry, spend your money, live to the hilt, don't worry about tomorrow and … buy my shoes. A basically permissive and hence surefire set of values.

Your success is exemplary. The proof is that you and your equals–I speak of corporations worthy of the name, which is to say the multinationals–today control most of the spending by indebted populations. And even beyond, since these populations do not hesitate to borrow in order to buy. You have taught them to behave with disconcerting docility and faithfulness.

I say "you," but my own name also figures on this prestigious list of grandmasters of perception engineering because I have advised hundreds of companies like yours over the last forty years. With immense success, I might add, seeing that you have called on me today.

Your company has therefore manufactured its own customers, and with remarkable efficiency since you have even succeeded in overturning a deeply entrenched behaviour. Fifty years ago, people went without clothes in order to eat. Today, people gladly go without food in order to buy clothes. And they do it again to fit inside them! It's really fantastic. I say so because I think so.

Will you allow me another little parenthetical remark? Thank you. I shall be brief.

It has often been said that the automobile is the invention that has had the greatest influence on the twentieth century. That it has changed the world by providing mobility. I am not of this opinion. I think the most significant invention of the century was the consumer: mass produced, the way Mr. Ford turned out his cars. The fact that mail-order sales outweighed car pickup services supports my position.

But I digress. Forgive me.

I was saying that your product is not so much the shoe as the individual who wears it. Despite the success for which I was complimenting you moments ago, therein, however, lies your weakness. The work that's so important to you is not only unfinished; you could very soon lose control of it. You're past masters at the manufacture of shoes, brands, and reputations, I grant you that. However, you haven't yet completely mastered the manufacture of individuals, which is an art. You're soft, hesitant, scrupulous. The consequence is this: unless you quickly adjust your sights, this is unquestionably where the enemy you have scented on the wind will come from. This enemy is the individual who buys your shoes and whom you have neglected to nudge along paths that will favour your growth.

Mr. President, you know as well as I do that this country is no longer run by its elected representatives. You yourself belong to a group of business leaders who map out and dictate economic and social policy. Every year, among a small, private inner circle, you decide which will be the next victims of your growth. Nothing escapes your scrutiny: rates of inflation, interest and unemployment, budgets of nations, average incomes, bank investments in corporations, takeovers, etc. The affairs of State are your affairs, so to speak. Which is perfectly normal since you're the ones who manufacture most of the State's citizens. Since the citizens are your products, you have every right to decide how they should be governed. You'll forgive me for speaking sharply, but as company executives you have been much too lax.

History has never really been something I've paid much attention to. Making one's living rummaging around in the past has always seemed profoundly retrograde to me. I've told you already that my affinities lie with those who move ahead. Nevertheless, I must draw your attention to the fact that all the empires in History crumbled when their emperors erred through overconfidence, and hence through blindness. Look at the Roman Empire. From the minute these empires considered the battle won, they lost control of their growth and let mildew grow on the walls of their institutions and even their palaces. Like you, they built brands and reputations and then model citizens. But like you, they turned soft. Thus empires crumbled, and I am here before you today to keep you from falling into the same trap.

In recent years, in order to ensure your growth, you of the big business community have worked to reduce both the number of your employees and the pay of those you have kept. For obvious reasons of cost reduction and profitability, you are gradually removing all those of the so-called "middle" class from your many companies.

I can only compliment you on this, for the middle class has been increasingly inconvenient. We know today that this invention of recent date, having appeared early in the last century, would not long be compatible with evolution and economic growth. It's much too demanding and much too expensive for companies and the various strata of society alike. Political leaders have been very naïve to think, and to lead people at large to think, that everyone would eventually live in a certain degree of comfort, gradually moving toward the so-called leisure society.

We've seen captains scuttle their own ships, but never as unconscionably as this.

The same aberration is obvious when we analyze the evolution of States. You'll agree with me that only one situation is propitious for growth, the one in which great, economically powerful nations are surrounded by tiny ones dedicated to serving them. Middle-sized nations are also recent inventions and have no future. With no doubt at all we will return to a world that obeys the laws of nature, with the strong on one side and the weak on the other, separated by a very narrow line because anything in between is much too rebellious.

The trouble with being in the middle is that it's never the right place. You'll either be too weak to be strong, or too strong to be weak. Ignoring this lesson of History will have you struggling against nature and against growth as well. You'll expend energy and never produce anything, unless it's pretentious, sometimes even arrogant populations, which will support a few inspired artists and a few too-obliging rebels. And even these will serve you one day and obstruct you the next.

But we'll leave States aside and come back to the middle class that has been fattening on your largesse over recent decades. You have at last undertaken to eliminate it, and that is very good. High time, I'd even say. A large proportion of the planet's problems arise directly from its condescending existence and the way in which it slows economic development with massive social demands. Once this class of deficients has vanished, societies will finally be able to achieve maturity and stability.

However, the elimination of this category of citizens, necessary as it is to the growth of your profits, raises a question to which you have not yet found an answer. I refer to its replacement.

This is precisely the problem I have been pondering over these recent months while you have been managing your day-to-day business.

The entire problem stems from the fact that the customers you have manufactured in the past few decades belong to the class you are now working to destroy. Look at your payroll today and compare it to similar payrolls twenty years ago. Compare them in current dollars, of course. What is unmistakable, and you have observed it, I hope, is the ultra-fast polarization of pay scales into two categories: high and low. For reasons of profitability, you are gradually eliminating all those in between, as we were saying a few minutes ago. Evolution could not proceed otherwise, of course. Except that you continue meanwhile to manufacture shoes intended for this vanishing class and also continue to manufacture your customers to have the consumer reflexes of this undesirable class. Even though your customers are going to be increasingly low earners, you blindly keep teaching them to think like the customers they will very soon no longer be. Decidedly, you're shooting yourselves in the foot!

If you were the only company to be dispensing with all these people who have clearly been earning too much money, you'd have no problem. But look around you, Mr. President. Look at the companies in the automobile sector, and furniture, and food. Companies everywhere are activating the same strategy of downward levelling. Their necessary and legitimate goal of profitability is gobbling up the middle class, which happens to be their primary source of earnings, yet they don't even give a thought to its replacement.

Who is going to buy your shoes tomorrow, then? The low earners. Inevitably. And if you keep on making shoes for them that they soon won't be able to afford, how the devil are you going to raise your profits and face your shareholders? Let's be real. They'll have your hides!

You'll protest, of course. You're going to give me the argument that yesterday you were still serving your shareholders. Moving your factories to low-pay countries lets you manufacture today at much lower cost, so your growth is guaranteed even with reductions in the price of your shoes and in numbers of units sold. To this you'll add the positions you've taken in other companies favourably placed vertically and horizontally, which steadies your profit figures, your margins, and so on and so forth.

Nonsense, Mr. President. Nonsense. I'm truly sorry, but the only thing I can tell you is that it's all nonsense.

Even if its profits increase, a company that cuts both its prices and its sales volume is managing its growth in reverse. It's a company living on borrowed time. Add a disappearing customer base, and you have a company headed for extinction.

Excuse my churlishness, but you know what I'm like, and you know I say what I think. I'm not the sort to tell you you're wearing a great hat if the hat makes me want to puke, and I would not be doing you a service if I lied about the fragility of your present and future situation, in case you should decide to disregard my warning and reject the application of the appropriate medicine.

I'll put the question again: who are your customers of tomorrow going to be? At the present time you have chosen not to think about the answer, Mr. President. That's why you're afraid. And why you're shaking in your own shoes.

But I've been thinking about it, Mr. President. And it's to deliver the consumers of tomorrow to you, bound hand and foot, that I've come back to appear before you and your fucking specialists. Yes, fucking specialists. I'm saying it bluntly. These people around you, Mr. President, whom you pay ten times the average you pay your employees–the ones in this country, of course. The only colour these people can see is the colour of the money you give them. With great gobs of financial planning full of errors and falsehoods based on models and suppositions dredged up out of fiction, they feed the illusion that everything's fine. The figures they calculate have no relation to anything but their wish not to wake the menace that's rumbling around the place where they've comfortably parked their rears.

What I'm saying hurts, of course. I can see you all steaming because you know I'm talking precisely about you who are here. Don't think I look down on you. Accept this tongue-lashing as a mark of my most profound respect instead because the blindness I'm accusing you of proves your dedication to the company. Your role is to manage this ship with the greatest loyalty to your captain. If your captain tells you to steer to starboard, it would be inappropriate and frowned upon to steer to port.

Would it be your fault, then, Mr. President, if this ship was sailing to its doom? Not yours either. There's no fog on the sea where you're sailing, and all around, the other transatlantic vessels are visible sailing in the same direction. How could you suspect that the precious spices lie on the other side? Anyway, the Earth is round, isn't it? In the worst of cases, you'd just make a detour. Like everyone else. Which is surely a comforting thought.

Mr. President, neither you nor the members of your Board are responsible for this situation. If companies like yours don't see the threat, it's quite simply because their real bosses, who are their shareholders, don't want to see it. The very thought that you could report negative returns gives them goosebumps, which gives you goosebumps by contagion. The result is that you charge head down at a wall that's going to smash your heads apart. The process has already begun, in fact. Companies are dying of an incurable disease called camouflage. Others are dying of a disease that's just as lethal called a sense of infallibility.

What do you want to die of? Tell me. I'll show you the shortest route. I know them all. I could even give you a precise and complete list of companies that are going to file for bankruptcy tomorrow. In alphabetical or obituarial order. Take your pick.

Of course, you'd rather not be on this list (I amused myself drawing it up during my pleasant little stay on my island). If so, prepare to make some dramatic changes in your practices. How? That is what we shall soon be talking about.

Madam, I see that you have picked up your pencil. I wish to tell you that you displease me in the extreme. I'm very serious, you know.

Mr. President, may I ask you to intervene on my behalf? I told you a few minutes ago that I would not tolerate any note-taking whatever during my presentation. If you refuse to comply with this requirement, I shall withdraw without a moment's hesitation. By the window if I have to.

Thank you.

Before continuing, and constructing, I feel the need to do a bit more demolition. Not for the pleasure. I've passed the age of filling halls with manure and then growing my roses in it. It's because I doubt that you're going to understand the urgency of the situation unless I make efforts to show you what kind of graveyard you're heading for.

On what strategies are you resting your hopes that you will continue to have the lion's share of the very lucrative footwear market? On an illusion, in both accounting and demographics.

In domestic markets, you're relying on reducing your production costs in order to bring down the prices of your shoes and maintain adequate sales volumes. There will be deficiencies to be made up, of course, because your customers will get poorer at an increasing rate. That won't matter, you say, because at the same time you'll spend an increasing portion of your earnings on winning new foreign markets, whose size you estimate to be five, ten, a hundred times occidental markets. Forgetting an essential element, however: that these new markets comprise only penniless people, whose reflexes you have no idea how to build, and gaining access to them will cost you five, ten, a hundred times your planned investments. Here, you're going to get mired as you'd never have suspected. To say it will be your Vietnam is an understatement.

At the head table at the annual party thrown by your private businessmen's club (a circle where one doesn't open one's own oysters), you've bragged about having made your first inroads in this or that hitherto virgin country where the head count is estimated in hundreds of millions—each head being joined to two feet, for your shoes. Good for you and good luck. Because before even one percent of these heads is trained and branded as yours, you'll have spent the profits earned on tens of millions of occidental heads. And it will be your embarrassing duty to inform your shareholders that in the end this very promising country can only be counted on for a very small number of people able and willing to pay for the shoes that the worker here, bled dry though he is, can still afford.

Pardon my arrogance, Mr. President, but wasn't it you who bragged last year about having transferred half your factories to countries where wages were costing you only a few shoelaces a month? Your shareholders must have given you a standing ovation. Can you explain to me now what those close-to-no-wage-earners are going to use for money to buy your shoes, since they're the new consumers you're counting on to make up for your lower earnings on domestic markets?

Mr. President, your company is in crisis because you have neglected to make your products fit your customers and your customers fit your products. You're behaving as though the one were not made for the other. How could you overlook, to such a degree, in its noblest manifestation, the first law of existence—the law of supply and demand?

Fortunately, the lifebuoy you need is here before you. A pretentious, arrogant, conceited one, but a lifebuoy, and no doubt the only one there is.

I hope you will reach out and take it.

HOW many years have we known each other, Mr. President? Over fifteen years, I believe. No? Oh yes, I assure you. The first time we met was the year your daughter entered the Conservatory. What idiocy that was. To learn to be a star, she should have registered in a school of commerce.

Do you remember what briefcase I was using at that time to carry my precious papers in? Wasn't it … this one? Yes, Mr. President, it really was this one. Not one like it–this one. Precisely this one. This briefcase has been with me everywhere for nearly thirty years. Would you be surprised now to hear that the company that made it closed its doors long ago?

Why?

I'll give you a clue. How many more briefcases do you think it would have sold me if it had survived until today? Three? Four? Ten? You're nowhere near. It wouldn't have sold me a single one because I still have the one that it made, and that I bought, nearly thirty years ago. It closed its doors because the products it made were too good. Their quality and appearance were both eternal. That's why the company went bankrupt, and that's the whole problem with your shoes.

I'm not saying your shoes are eternal, or that I could be wearing the pair I buy from you today thirty years from now. I'm drawing your attention to this briefcase that destroyed its manufacturer to convince you of the reason for the very first change you must make for the years to come: you must turn shoes into perishable goods.

Like pastries.

One of the most brilliant inventions of the last hundred years, dear friends, is the garbage bag. Imagine. People buy bags for the exact and premeditated purpose of throwing them out. They buy garbage. And what do they do when they've thrown them all out? They buy more. And throw those out, and on and on. It's fascinating, don't you think? What an extraordinary invention! This is exactly what you must do from now on. Sell shoes meant to be thrown out.

I was saying minutes ago that your products were far less the shoes people wear than the people who wear them. You're cutting their pay to maintain your margins? That's a measure I can only approve. However, now you'll have to make sure you don't sell them briefcases like the one I still have, but garbage bags. It's as plain as could be.

You were saying, Sir? Consumers will never buy poor quality shoes? You're absolutely right. And why, I ask you? For one reason and only one: at present they buy shoes expecting to keep them a long time. It's a simple matter of perception, and it's precisely on this score that you must step in. The aim of this second change will be to convince consumers that shoes are no longer meant to be worn for years. You must change their way of thinking about them: shoes must become pastries, things that don't last. Unless you get into the world of fast consumption and disposable goods immediately, it will cost you dearly. For with the pay cuts you're putting through, at the present price of your shoes your customers soon won't be able to pay enough for them to fill your shareholders' bellies.

You're smiling, I see, Madam. Yes, you, who wouldn't put down your pencil a little while ago. In your place I would hold back that condescending smirk of make-believe queen and real marionette. It gives away your difficulty understanding what I'm talking about. Because tomorrow your superior (I'd even say, "vastly superior") will most probably hand you this company's most important responsibility, which is to carry out the change of direction whose absolute necessity I'm talking myself hoarse explaining. Why you? Because women and disposable things are made for each other. You ladies can't wait for disposable shoes to become the norm. You've been working toward it for years. You won't admit it, of course, but you're queens of all that's here today and gone tomorrow, and your greatest joy isn't buying something, but buying, period. Opening the jaws of your croco purse as often as possible and biting into whatever gives you an itch in the stores. This company will soon rationalize your buying all the shoes you want, and you'll love it because you'll be relieved of justifying a reflex that troubles you on the surface but in your heart of hearts makes you happy.

You must thank heaven, furthermore, that you make your living in footwear. It's one of the most conservative and cautious economic sectors I know. One only has to look at production figures for the past hundred years to realize how little the industry has evolved. Laces are given up for straps, then straps for laces. Heels are raised, then lowered. We go from leather to suede, then from suede to leather. We go from black to red, then from red to black. And thereupon the history of footwear is complete.

Oh, it's not your fault the footwear industry has such slippered, stay-at-home habits. In a world of quality and durability, there are constraints of all kinds. Mind you, that's a very good thing because this long stretch of drowsiness will let you offer consumers some brand new market excitement. There will be lots of room for imagination, and we all know that where there's innovation, there's a future. Anyone who's quick on his feet can live at least half a century on a single innovation. We'll have several of them.

Take just one of the characteristics inherent in footwear: its specific function. Today there are shoes for sports, others for special occasions, meaning for show, then still others for every day. Isn't it wonderful news that, with agreement right here, together, on the day when shoes become disposable, we might see this classification explode, spawning a multitude of models with far more specific functions? In future we might offer lively and expressive shoes that tell everyone that we're at a certain point of the week, or even of the day.

Apparel has long been the art of appearance, identity, and belonging. This is not new. The way one dresses is essentially a language. I can dress as a businessman, an intellectual, a sportsman, or a Don Juan. In this way, I can say clearly and without opening my mouth that I'm a businessman, an intellectual, a sportsman, or a Don Juan. The codifications are clear, sure enough, but so limited! Once footwear is freed of its obligation to be durable, it will enrich this vocabulary. We'll be able to develop a complex language expressing personalities, states of mind, and moods. You wake up in the morning with a mad desire to be a race-car driver? A shoe will be clearly identified with this mad passion. You're tired and want to spend your day under a tree watching the birds? Another shoe will signal, "Bug off, leave me alone!" You wake up feeling great and determined to have a drink with everyone you know? This will be clearly indicated by another shoe you'll wear so all your friends will know at first sight.

I know you're amused by the description I've just given you. I'm quite serious, though. At the moment, people who love car racing don't have special shoes. They wear "baskets," as the French call them, though most race buffs have a mortal horror of basketball. And all other sports too. Associating a shoe with a car race is unthinkable today because these circuses don't last longer than three days. No one would buy the F1 shoe because it couldn't be worn long enough to justify buying it. But if it were designed, manufactured, and sold to be worn for three days and then thrown away the fourth, it would be quite another thing. Admit it. You'd sell considerable quantities to consumers who would put those shoes in the garbage the fourth day and get new ones. Without a single hesitation because no one would want them any more anyway, the race and excitement being things of the past.

In a world that cultivates disposable personalities, footwear meant for specific and passing use will be both a necessity and a huge relief, not a whim or a luxury. This is nothing less than the recipe for short, medium, and long-term profitability. It will open the door to a vast market by reconciling two things: need and desire. The need to wear shoes and the desire to keep buying.

The possibilities are infinite because to uses we'll add moods. Personal and social moods. Once in a while,

Mr. President, don't you get up in the morning wanting no one to say a word to you? If a shoe could signal this to your entourage, you would no doubt be very cross not to have a pair at hand, or rather, ready to put on your feet that day when you dread the mere courtesy of saying good morning to your neighbour. Think now of all those single men and women who wake up in their beds alone in the morning and swear not to go to bed alone in them that night. Prowling shoes for lonesome singles will make for some happy people … in pairs.

No, Madam. No, Sir. All this is not a laughing matter. Shoes have very long since left the world of utility and comfort for the world of appearance. Very long since. The one and only thing that keeps them from joining the world of makeup and perfume, which one can change at any hour of the day or night and thus adapt to our moods, is their durability, and therefore their price. You must break this mould.

I see by your faces that you've already stopped listening to me. You're all buried in learned calculations, trying to figure out how you can manufacture shoes at low enough cost to sell them at high volume and at the price of a pastry that will fatten only your bottom line.

Be assured that I have a solution to this problem. And to all the others besides. Would you dare think, as real as I am before you at this very minute, that I could propose strategies to you whose intelligence, feasibility, and profitability I haven't checked out and confirmed?

It's incredibly simple, however. All you need is to develop a universal, strong, durable, high-quality sole on which it will be possible to mount a cheap, removable showpiece upper. Admit it's worth thinking about. This sole will be of the quality of my briefcase, the one I have with me, that I was talking about a few minutes ago. The showy upper will be of low quality because that's what will be bought to be transitory, like pastries, to be thrown away, like garbage bags.

This sole will not be complicated to develop. Today there are materials that are very durable and will surely be very comfortable. What will be important is to design the most effective system of attachment, and then patent it all. Considering your connections, this last should only be a formality.

There will be development costs, of course. I'm sure your banker will be delighted to arrange things. He'll have the perfect pretext for transferring your company to the list of high-risk clients, after which he'll turn your file over to his son, who will build himself a reputation for good management as easily as falling off a log. Daddy may hand him the chairmanship of the Board, then make him President and CEO. That's what's called natural selection.

You'll have realized that the sole, contrary to its decoration, will allow for no gimmickry, no taste, no desirability, and above all no variation. Esthetically, it must absolutely take a back seat. It must be only the dumb, colourless stem that holds the flower. If this sole had to be available in different colours and different styles, you would damage your own efforts and be back to square one. This is why it's important, I repeat, to patent it in all its ugliness.

Then, Mr. President, you must lead a relentless campaign to have shoes sold henceforth in food stores, and especially in the perishable goods department, so as to associate them not just with the seasons but with the appetites of the day. You must make sure that the models don't stay on the shelves more than two weeks and are replaced by new, always different ones. Your customers will be delighted they're not durable because they'll hate to have to throw them away still fresh.

You were saying? You still doubt our ability to change people's mentalities? That shows you don't really know human nature, Sir. Put any individual before two pairs of shoes. The first pair costs $120, and that's a good price, and the second costs $3. Yes, I did say $3. Which will he take? Tomorrow, we'll have conditioned him as easily as can be to take the pair at $3. Even if the word "Disposable" is printed on the label in big, very red letters. Why? Because, besides only paying $3 for those shoes, he knows he can throw them away in a few days and come and pick out another pair in a different model. He won't have to live with the same model for several months. He can follow his daily moods and thereby assert himself fully.

Don't forget that men and women of today are accomplished consumers. They're nothing else, in fact, because they've grown up with that reflex. To them, nothing is more pleasing and satisfying than buying. Let them buy more often and they'll be enchanted. Offer them a bonus in the possibility of changing personality every day and they'll kiss your feet. Disposable shoes will be the answer to one of the most widespread desires among our contemporaries: the ability to make regular personality changes. And treat themselves to the ultimate bliss besides. Have you already forgotten that tomorrow's consumer will be penniless? Disposable shoes will make him spend to your advantage as well as make him forget that it was you who destroyed his buying power. Shouldn't that be called genius?

Your fashion designers will be delighted with this change of direction. And you'll have to allow them all the necessary scope for inspiration. On the other hand, you'll have to make them stop taking their inspiration from international fashion trends led by the idle rich of our time and start getting it from the tabloids' incoherent editorials, weather forecasts, lonely hearts letters, Flo-Flo's astrological columns, the latest gossip over movie stars, and all that crap that feeds the humours and opinions of daily life. You have to tell them to take shoes out of the world of fashion and put them into the world of the instant, of here today, gone tomorrow, of disposable thinking, the kind dictated by the prefabricated illusions of our time.

I don't doubt your executives' sterling qualities for an instant. All the same, make sure that those who supervise the work of your designers thoroughly understand the importance of having a team much more attuned to the music of the street than to the art taught by the great fashion schools. These people should above all know first-hand what goes on in the cities, streets, and lanes. See and understand real life.

They should be fuelled by the spectacle of all the trash begging along the sidewalks. After all, it's the sight of this decay that lets people these days believe they still have a certain dignity. Having others beg will soon be their greatest wealth. Your executives must be aware of this in order to direct their teams.

On this score, the music of the street is far richer than you think. Unlike the music of entertainment experts, it alone sings with mouthfuls of dust raised by passing trucks, motorcycles, and mediocrity. It doesn't sing of dreams, it shouts the truth. This is why, for you and me, it's so hard to listen to. The street will be the most prolific source of inspiration for the designers of disposable shoes, the shoes of real life, the life of tomorrow, which will know only what is now, and–this I must stress–will never be anything but an eternal survival.

I am not a specialist in shapes, motifs, and colours. However, my understanding of consumer reflexes being legendary, I feel entitled to proffer some points of advice to these designers. What they absolutely must understand is that consumer attitudes of tomorrow will be closely associated with a new value–negation.

Yes, Madam, negation.

When you see young people around you piercing new orifices all over their faces and bodies to hold worthless trinkets, when you see the same young people listening to bellowings in the guise of music and spending fortunes on passing pleasures like movies, it really is blind not to see and understand the society of tomorrow in it all–a society that will strive by every means to leave reality and arrive at make-believe.

If you're surprised by what I'm saying, dear friends, it's because you don't come down from your tower often enough. It's characteristic of today's managers to imagine they know people just because they eat at Chinatown's most highly regarded restaurants. But since when do good Chinese restaurants make fortunes by feeding the man in the street? They feed people like you, for heaven's sake. They're excellent merchants.

You don't know today's consumer, Mr. President, because you rub shoulders with him only through intermediaries, your marketing strategists. But these people eat in the same restaurants you do. They live in the same world as you and your close associates. Enviously, of course. And you pay them to tell you what you want to hear, with the result that the chasm between you and reality gets deeper.

Will you allow me to describe this consumer, the one of today and the one of tomorrow? I warn you, you're going to be astounded, positively astounded. This consumer is none other than the one you yourselves have built over the years, in fact, you and your kind, meaning all those companies with their eyes riveted on quick profits. You built your consumers to suit your needs, of course, but you never bothered about what would happen to them later, the secondary effects, the long-term consequences. And there's your whole problem. Because you're making shoes for them now without knowing how to get them to buy those shoes tomorrow.

I won't hide from you that this morning I still wasn't sure I should describe these consumers to you. What if you didn't understand? Worse, what if you didn't believe me? I'm still very much afraid I'll have to backtrack and keep the remaining portion of my presentation for later. A few years later. Until the day when you'll be faced with fact, and at the same time you'll be powerless to act because it will be too late.

I decided to go ahead. Will you make the effort to put aside life as you know it, the life you grew up in, and follow what I have to say unconditionally? It will be to your advantage because otherwise I shall pack up and leave. In plain language, I'm asking you to follow me and forget what you've always taken for granted.

Listen carefully. All you risk is to learn.

—•—

A FEW years ago, consumers—your customers—had values based on hope. Most had inherited them from the different religions, naturally, since religions have always specialized in dreams. Imagine, in no time at all, these values were replaced by their opposites through a very simple effect of flipping from the real world to the virtual world.

So that you'll properly understand this phenomenon, which I can see escapes you, let me illustrate it with a metaphor.

This exercise will demand a certain effort on your part, Madam. I apologize in advance. I know you're unaccustomed to it.

Imagine for a moment that you're in a plane, Mr. President. You're comfortably seated, in first class, and you're glancing at the newspaper while you finish your breakfast. You look at your watch; you still have three hours to kill. The hostess serves you a second coffee, which tastes of nothing but the sugar you've put in it. You look at the clouds for a while, then—well now! A movie. OK, why not. But it's a really awful movie. As usual, a kind of science-fiction western with Don Juans duelling with light sabres for a woman's ass. So you fall asleep.

An hour later, maybe two, you've no idea how long, you wake suddenly because someone's shaking you hard and holding out a backpack, shouting that the engines are on fire. You barely realize what's happening when you're told you have to choose between two things: either fasten your seatbelt and hope to come out alive from an uncontrolled landing, or jump with this backpack, which is a parachute, which you have to open by pulling hard, here, on this cord.

Of course, you panic. Especially because there's thick smoke hurting your eyes. A smell of burning rubber begins to turn your stomach till your head swims. You look through the window and see that you're no longer over the ocean, and at the same time you realize that the plane is descending fast. It's not just gliding any more. You'll have to have a lot of courage to jump out of this machine because jumping out into space is not an easy thing to do. But do you have a choice? So you jump.

That's done it, you're falling through thin air. It's horrible. Really horrible. You didn't even like the height from your office window. Now you think you're going to die of fright. Oh, there's the parachute! Is it well attached? Who's going to open it? Ah, yes, it's you. They told you to pull on this cord, here, in front. So quick, you pull, and slap! The parachute opens. It gives you a great jolt but … what a relief to feel the freefall change abruptly to a descent that you know is slower.

At last you can breathe. The descent is long, and you realize in the end it's rather pleasant compared to what you'd thought at first. In fact, it's not really so long, but the moment seems an eternity. It's the contrast. Contrast between the gentleness of this descent and the violence before because the freefall was truly appalling. From the moment you jumped to the moment your parachute opened, you really thought this was the end. That you were finished. That you were going to smash into the ground, or die of fright before ever getting there.

Now that the descent is gentler, slower, you have time. Yes, time. To think. You have a strange feeling besides that you're thinking for the first time in years. You've just died and been reborn in the space of a few seconds, and it's this you're thinking about. You look at the sky, then you look down at the Earth you're approaching. You feel a kind of light-headed joy. You're surprised to find yourself laughing. It's a nervous laugh, to be sure, but you're laughing. You've just jumped into thin air, but you're laughing.

You'd like this moment to last an eternity. More than that, you'd like the parachute not to have opened yet so you could still be experiencing that freefall, but better. The memory is already no longer one of horror but of a moment of excess. To tell the truth, you'd like to be afraid again. For the pleasure of controlling that fear. Of living it with rage and aggression in place of dread.

A dramatic turn: you wake up. Your absurd reaction is to cling firmly to your seat. As if you'd just lost your balance and were going to fall. What's happening? What has happened? You had a dream, that's all. You're still in the plane. Your heart's beating so hard you can hear it in your ears. What a horrible dream! But at the same time, what a fantastic experience! For a moment, you lived through something you never imagined possible: a leap into thin air that was positively intoxicating.

Mr. President, after centuries and centuries of uneventful flights, apart from a few minor bumps, our society today is an aeroplane in flames. No one knows what will become of it, but from now on one thing is certain: hope and the future can no longer justify the existence of any values whatsoever beyond those intimately tied to the ecstasy of the present. Nobody looks up any more. Everybody looks down.

To keep the confidence of our passengers as long as possible, to distract them, to keep them from panicking, and of course keep them from taking umbrage at us, the pilots, we give them parachutes. Even better, we get to sell them parachutes. Like those companies that sell both gas and gas masks, mines and mine detectors, missiles and anti-missile canons. With the magic we're capable of, we sell them parachutes with such conviction that they stay calm as can be. They're even in a hurry to jump. And they do. Some even jump without a parachute, Mr. President. Without a parachute, they want so badly to live to the full, the promised ecstasy created by us so they can enjoy life without thinking about the fire that's destroying our aeroplane.

Mr. President, society has flipped from real to virtual with complicity from us with our aptitude, but also and above all it was urgent and imperative that we create a semblance of happiness to protect ourselves from rebellion.

This is what we call sublimation. Sublimation of reality, which has given birth to the virtual. The real world, the one I reconnected with in Greece, is a world in the image of all the animal and vegetable species that we know have disappeared. It exists only in memory. This world itself is disappearing gradually, giving way to the virtual world, the one in which imagination is born of reality's disintegration.

In the space of a few years, a very few years, the consumer has flipped. And we are the ones who have made him do it. For our own safety, we have talked up the virtues of our parachutes to him. He likes jumping. He asks for more. As soon as he's on the ground, he climbs back in the plane so he can jump again.

This leap into thin air takes the most varied forms, and my own premise is the point of departure and justification for all of them. I spoke about this premise of mine when I introduced myself to you this morning. I refer of course to an absence of scruples. I myself am old and have no future. Young people, who theoretically have a future, behave exactly as I do. Is it I who am still young, or they who are already old? The result is the same. Neither they nor I care in the least what tomorrow will bring. Nor even confidence that there will be a tomorrow.

That too, Mr. President, is in the order of sublimation. And if you want my opinion, it's an exceptional phenomenon in the history of humanity. Man, and you too, Madam, considers today that he is an endangered species. And that it's quite simply the way it is, and we don't need to get in a stew about it.

If you think I'm about to shed tears over this, you're wrong. I see not just a marvellous opportunity for companies like yours in this evolution of our societies, but also the birth of an era for which I'd give up my wealth and my reputation too if it could only offer the chance of rebirth to me as well.

I'll go further, Mr. President. At the risk of shocking you really deeply, I'll tell you that, without even realizing it ourselves, we've transformed consumers to be just like us, and to think just like us.

You won't deny that the ultimate reason you keep wanting to grow is that day by day you want to get more independent of money. Your wealth allows you to go to bed at night confident that nothing on this Earth could prevent you from living exactly the way you want, free of all obligation, even of having to work for your living. But every morning, you go to work anyway. Why? Because what's important to you isn't being able to live without working. You'd die of boredom. It's knowing you *could* live without working. We have taught the young people of today, however, that it's altogether possible to live fully and intensely, even without a penny. Giving no thought whatever to the morrow, in other words. As if they, like you, were independent of money.

You of another generation wouldn't be capable of living calmly and coolly without a fat fortune in your bank accounts. Today's consumers do it as easily as can be, and without a penny. Why? Because, by offering them so many artificial versions of paradise and so many virtual lives, you've taught them that the intensity of life doesn't depend on much and certainly not on moolah.

Film and music have been highly effective instruments in the creation of this new, all virtual way of life that's a long, long way from reality. They succeed in turning us into heroes of every kind, and create worlds for us in which sensations are stronger and stronger and more and more realistic. By offering us dreams that keep getting more exhilarating, more fleeting, and so much more thrilling, they tear us away from the monotony and worries of our daily lives.

Tomorrow no longer exists, Mr. President. Nor does hope. From now on, all that exists is today, the present moment. Hence the unassailable certainty that shoes must be disposable if they're going to be part of this moment, this ecstasy, this rebirth of human grandeur.

You persist in selling your shoes to ants when your customers are cicadas today. Yesterday's values don't hold any more because everyone knows the plane is on fire. Nobody's betting on a soft landing. I'd even say categorically that at the rate things are going, none of the passengers want that landing. The parachute jumping gets them so excited, so turned on. Why land when we can throw ourselves out into space and get all those sensations? Why cling to that plane when we know that even if we survive the landing it'll be in a mangled mess, you companies will have taken so much of everything from us?

Technology has created such fascinating worlds that reality has become a by-product of virtuality. We live in reality only to respond to our basic needs. One of the most eloquent illustrations is the way we eat. We don't eat: we ingurgitate. The number of hamburgers produced and ingurgitated yearly would persuade anyone to invest in mustard. Also in stomach-soother pills.

There's more. Since we first invented consumption, we've relentlessly associated it with self-assertion, selling everything with phrases calculated to hammer home the idea that buying brings possession, which leads to giving oneself an existence, power, superiority. Well, those days are over. Already, that doesn't work any more. The consumer has fully entered a postcommercial phase and soon he'll buy only to the extent that he feels he's not asserting his identity by doing it, but dissolving in the shifting sands of self-destruction. Buying will be an act of protest. Against whom? Against what? Against consumption. Rational consumption, Mr. President, which yesterday made him rich and today makes him poor.

Your customer is no fool. He knows very well that if he loses his job, or if he keeps it in exchange for less pay, it's because you keep getting greedier. I was telling you not long ago that you had been too soft. That you had been letting things go, like an overconfident emperor. Now you'll reap the consequence of your clumsiness. You'll have to make some very quick adjustments: the enemy is at your gates.

As long as you were allowing this customer to think he could exist in this society, be someone, make his place in it and even influence it, selling him hope, self-assertion, and good humour was effective and profitable. Tomorrow, anyone who thinks this place in the sun can still exist will be laughed out of town. Everyone will know that the dream is over. There will be gloom on all faces. If the consumer is going to keep buying and buying in this society that has betrayed him, if he's going to smile his customer's smile again, you're going to have to sell him the idea that buying your shoes tallies with self-assertion in its noblest and most rapturous form to suit his anti-values: jumping into thin air, self-assertion by negation.

I confess to some pride, Mr. President, in having understood something Caesar himself only half understood. Faced with grumbling from his people, the emperor proclaimed "Bread and games" as the remedy. What I have understood, and what I am sharing with you today, is that your growth depends on your capacity to offer more and more games. Why? Because bread is getting more and more expensive. So the more games there are, the less bread there will have to be.

Open your eyes and observe with me that there now exist two categories of individuals. Recognizing and understanding them is basic to the strategy you will need to deploy.

No, Sir. No, Sir. It's not a question of rich and poor. Already there are not enough rich people, those who have done well financially, to form a category. The two categories I'm talking about are first, people who dream of living, and second, people who live on dreams.

The first are those who at this very moment are walking about with placards on which they're sounding the alarm and venting their outrage. There aren't many of them, but they're all over the place. They organize in small groups so they can cover all territories. They're against companies, against governments, and even against the century. Their self-assertion consists of denying your right to life: these people want to destroy companies whom they accuse of destroying their freedom. These new poor people dream of recovering their privileges and will spend the rest of their days dreaming of it. You and I know that day will never come–there can't be any question of turning back and decommercializing human life. Our societies wouldn't get over it. Fighting progress is fighting against History.

As few as there are of this category at present, however, their number is growing alarmingly. Their laments are contagious. These people are dangerous because increasingly they're using your weapons and fighting on your turf. In their ranks you find lawyers, economists, and even strategists trained in my school. They've taken it into their heads to use all means to undermine your progress. They base their demands on all those things they call the evils of the century, which are in fact only the normal marks of an evolution that has simply passed them by. They denounce the exploitation of natural resources as if oil and trees were historic monuments; they protest against economic globalization as if stagnating companies could be sure to get them jobs; they protest against the automation of production whereas their grandfathers battled exploitation of their muscles; and they find fault with biogenetic progress while lamenting the fate of people dying of hunger.

Their contradictions are obvious, but they are skilled at waking in their kind the sleeping taste for revolution in all of us. Who hasn't dreamed of being at the storming of the Bastille? Or the October Revolution? In tourist mode, of course. So they pounce on every opportunity to recreate minor versions of the May '68 Paris riots here and there, then they can talk about revolutions they haven't lived through. And they print little newspapers for themselves, give speeches to a few bystanders, and write books that the century's new martyrs will publish.

To be a thousand, all they need to have is a hundred. They've all got a spoon and a pot, which makes ten times more noise. That said, fortunately, out of those hundred pots, you'll find ninety who are only there for the fun and to make a noise. On condition it doesn't rain, of course. Or it's not too cold. As soon as the party's over, they hurry back to join the others in this second category I'm about to describe–those you still controlled yesterday, but who are beginning to get away from you.

This second category comprises a very large majority. These people do not dream of living. We have taught them to live on dreams. They cling to these illusions, on account of the immense power of marketing, and people like me who protect your interests. They watch the first group parading around with their placards and graffiti, banging on their pots, and if they're tempted it's never for long. Between the so-called organic carrot and the hamburger with relish, mustard, and ketchup, between heavy, drab llama wool and synthetic fibres in the colours of life, between chamber music and metal-bending decibels, between books with endless sentences and fast-moving computer games, you can be sure they choose the pleasure of the moment, instant gratification, a high–the parachute I was talking about. All the things that let them live a dream, right now.

For how much longer? That depends entirely on you.

Your shoes should pitch the second group against the first, of course. They should help spread the idea that all long-range thinking must be shelved, not to speak of thinking of any kind. They should be a hymn to the beauty of the present, rebelling not against your companies but against this retrograde idea that you have to live for the future instead of right now. Thinking about the future means saving money in the present. This is an obstacle that puts a break on consumption, and you have to fight it.

If most people go for this new form of self-assertion, which consists of negating, it's because negation is one of the most natural things. When, I ask you, does a newborn begin to be human? From the moment he first says, "no." This "no" marks our arrival in the world. We could even say with certainty that negation is the very first of our self-assertions. In the cradle we were already asserting our preference for the present and our disregard for the future. The idea of worrying about our future is not a divinely natural one, however the priestly class may like it; it's essentially a cultural thing.

What I'm proposing to you here, today, is the acceleration of a commercial revolution that is already under way, and which must be emphasized. I hope you recognize both the value and the genius of this.

———•———

IN case you're hesitant to consider my advice, let me dangle the spectre of the worst you have to fear. As you know, my reputation is also based on the fact that I have always founded my strategies on strict analysis of what will happen to the client who does not apply them. Which is a characteristic of the most exacting and efficacious professionalism.

What will happen if you let things go? It's very simple, Mr. President. Very simple and at the same time tragic: in less than ten years you will be hanging at the end of a rope.

Well, I hear silence.

Listen carefully to what I'm going to say, Mr. President. And you too, Madam, and you too, Gentlemen. I'm not joking. And I remind you that I have no personal stake in being here today.

On behalf of your shareholders and as worthy heirs of your predecessors, you have been fattening your big companies by devouring the people. So be it. But today you have come to the top of this hitherto ascending curve. You are the pilots of this plane that's on fire. If you don't provide the most elating, desirable parachutes, you're going to crash along with your passengers.

What's more, you'll need to provide these parachutes immediately. Because while you're piloting this ill-fated craft, in the economy class in the rear, the pots are getting noisier and noisier. There are not many of them, but reliable information leads me to believe that they're regrouping and plan to seize the plane's flight control cabin. Attacking from all sides at once.

Revolutions, Mr. President, are always started by a handful of individuals. The longer you wait before acting, the harder it will be to stop them from advancing and achieving their ends.

You don't believe me?

When I came into your company's office building this morning, Mr. President, I had no intention of saddening you personally. I see that I must, however, and it will not be pleasant.

Your brother died eight years ago, Mr. President. He was devoured by the flesh-eating disease. The bacterium that causes it is a microscopic organism that reproduces in a mysterious way, and we have not yet learned how really to stop it. If it's diagnosed early, we can amputate the affected limb and be rid of it. At the price of the amputated limb. If it's recognized too late, it will eat you whole. Which is what happened to your brother. I'm sorry for reminding you of this very bad memory. I know how important your brother was to you.

A reminder of this tragic event is not pleasant, I grant you. May it help me convince you to consider my warnings most gravely. The grumbling from these consumers I've been calling pot-bangers is very real. And as few as they are, I know from experience that if you don't thwart their rebellion, you won't go down in History in the way you hope to. And when I tell you that you'll hang at the end of a rope, Mr. President, please believe that I couldn't be more serious. You'll hang on the rope that you'll have put round your own neck because you haven't been able to face the blow-up of your company and—worse still—your reputation.

I'm strongly tempted to give you a detailed description of the death-struggle you'll suffer soon and incurably unless you take the steps I prescribe. I shall do so later if necessary. In the hope it won't be. But I sense that I have now regained your full attention, and so I shall continue my presentation, pretending to believe that you're willingly following what I have to say. As long as I have your attention, I won't need to frighten you.

Disposable shoes will be ideal shoes for the rebel society, the one making itself heard, and that's heralding a new age in the history of humanity. Your guide in the manufacture of tomorrow's shoes, brands, reputations, and individuals should be the idea itself of consumption that says no, that firmly rejects consumption as it's known at present by choosing the trivial, the disposable, and that offers the possibility of buying any way one wants every three days. In other words, that gives the impression of not really consuming.

You won't have any trouble handling this because disposable thought has already begun to replace what went before it. Are you still worried about the lives your children and grandchildren will have, and the future of the planet, Mr. President? I'll be very surprised if you tell me you are. Without a moment's hesitation I'll call you a dinosaur, an old relic, or, worse still, an idealist. Pretty soon, thought is something we'll be stuffing and putting in museums and libraries, maybe even in bank vaults. Ideally in Swiss bank vaults so it'll never more see the light of day. For too long now, thought has only served to put a brake on our ambitions, keep us marking time rather than moving forward, put spokes in the wheels of progress and—worse still—deprive us of any gracious living by denying us our basic pleasures on the pretext of so-called civility, equality, or some kind of concern for the preservation of those tomorrows we won't give a fig about because we won't be there.

It's surprising to observe that man has succeeded in living as long as he has despite giving so much room to thought. We have been thinking for almost three centuries now. More precisely since the Enlightenment, whose thinkers, in my opinion, have only enlightened our contradictions. It's a long time, three centuries. Too long, even. It's high time we put an end to this tiresome habit and went back to healthier and more productive values.

I'm telling you, the day you put your essential thinking capacities into feet, you'll have settled two major problems. The thought problem, of course, but also the one about your shoes. People will walk in your footsteps.

I can hear your consultants crying shame all the way from here. These so-called specialists, who call themselves scientists so they can jack their fees, will tell you it's not enough to decide that shoes are going to be disposable to make a success of them. That brands are built at the cost of long months of research and market studies at $200 an hour so as to settle on the right design, the right material, and the right colour. They'll predict that without these things (which only they know how to conduct), no shoe will ever sell. These people are like your lawyers. They tell you that without them you can't move an inch without falling on your faces.

Mr. President, have you asked them how many shoes you'd sell if you didn't invest veritable fortunes in advertising? The truth, whether they like it or not, is that it's your expenditures on television, billboards, and fashion magazines that make your shoes so desirable. Withdraw the enormous budgets you give these supposed specialists in psychoconsumerism, hire the first ten people you meet up with in the street and put them at design tables, and every day you'll have prototypes for a hundred shoe models to fuel this strategy of marketing disposable shoes.

You will need not only to invent disposable shoes but make their virtues an obsession. How? By making real cult objects of these things we put our feet in. This is something you do already. Now you must make your cult a real phenomenon, so that the cult of shoes dominates all other cults in the look creation market.

Today, celebrities are the product of a studied package in which shoes occupy only one place in an array of elements of attraction. This place is shared by shoes with dresses, shirts, trousers, hairdos, and even makeup. You should work with urgency to make the choice of footwear the single valid measure of elegance and style, and hence social standing. Why? Because you will be imitated. Listen to my advice: begin now knocking dresses off the look creation market. Make sure that the future standard will be footwear. All discretionary income, instead of being shared with dresses or diluted in makeup base, will funnel toward your company.

Since all your models will be disposable and of little value, you'll sell them at carrot prices. Your shoes will be on the household grocery list, and every week each family member will need several pairs. And don't worry about their bulk because the materials used will make them pliable and compressible and they'll be sold in little boxes no bigger than sardine cans. All bearing the label, "recyclable," whether true or false: you'll agree that it's not the least important; the fines will always cost less than the development of biowhatzit materials.

Mr. President, I see that the lady who was reducing her chances of deserving your confidence a little while ago is now reducing her chances of even being taken seriously. I wouldn't wish to interfere in the management of your personnel, but if this picture of insipidity continues to show me disrespect, I suggest that she be hung on some other wall. I swear she's in the wrong room.

Let me tell you, Madam, that you will be the first to fill your grocery basket with these little boxes, which this company will soon be producing especially for you. Do you know why? Because, since your entire personality is in your feet, you are already a model of tomorrow's typical consumer.

Since the lady has volunteered, Mr. President, allow me to take her as an example of your customer of tomorrow.

Yesterday your company was still selling its shoes by selling a lifestyle that consisted essentially of being in style. It was the period when your customers, who had reasonable incomes, could pay for that style … and those shoes. Tomorrow, you're going to sell them the idea that only shoes are going to let them assert their rebellion. They'll be delighted since you're only going to ask a price they can afford.

This lady will buy three pairs of shoes a week because it will be the custom in the new society to change shoes three times a week. She will have to because you, Mr. President, will have imposed this way of thinking and she won't be able to do anything about it. A few years from now, you will have so influenced people's attitudes that it will become socially unacceptable, I repeat, unacceptable, not to change shoes regularly, for the simple reason that that's the way life will be.

Madam, a few years ago you were watching a science-fiction movie in which the characters were communicating by a network of computers. Bored by this crass nonsense invented by some perpetually infantile scatterbrain, you shut off the TV and leafed through a magazine in which you were shown primitive African tribespeople mutilating themselves in religious rites, men and women driving huge coloured rings through their noses. Disgusted with these two absurd voyages, one into the future and the other into the past, you shrugged your shoulders and went to bed.

Today, dear lady, I can supply you with Internet addresses where the whole on-line world can see young girls–including your daughter perhaps–posing nude with rings attached I won't say where because you would be revolted. Will you deny that things you took yesterday as too futuristic on the one hand, and too far in the past on the other, exist today? Will you deny the formidable power of someone with the will to impose his views? Will you deny that shoes will be sold tomorrow in little boxes in grocery stores … and that you'll buy them?

Everyone in this room takes at least a bath or a shower a day. Do you think people in the Middle Ages washed every day? What seems natural today was not natural yesterday, and what is not today will be tomorrow. It only needs to be decided upon. It is your duty to your shareholders, Mr. President, to have your Board decide that this lady be obliged to buy three pairs of shoes a week at $3 a pair. Failing which, your company won't even sell enough shoes to pay your own salary.

If your company made watches, I would tell you to impose disposable watches by cultivating the idea that personality is worn on one's wrist. But you make shoes. So I'm telling you that your salvation lies in your capacity to manage the personalities of people of tomorrow by persuading them that their personalities are in their feet, entirely in their feet, and only in their feet. You will need to convince consumers not to think with their heads any longer.

You're paying me so handsomely also, of course, to teach you how to go about it. You know as well as I do that how you go about it will decide how well you succeed, and your chances of making your success irreversible. And here, if I may say so, you'll once again have an opportunity to measure the extent of my genius. For the goal is ambitious, but the way of achieving it, which I'm about to reveal to you, is more astute than anything you have ever seen to this day. In a few years, Mr. President, people will associate you with the greatest minds of the century.

This subject will quickly become fascinating, but before getting into it I'm going to put a question to this audience. A very simple question but one to which very few people know the answer: in present-day consumption, which group of consumers has the real power?

Pardon? Pardon me, Sir, I didn't hear your reply. Those who still have money, you say? Wrong. Besides, there are already too few of them to exert any influence.

And you, Sir. What do you think? Childless couples? You're joking. They'll always be the most sheep-like people on earth. They pretend to be the century's forerunners, but they're not. They're happy enough following, conforming. They always want to wear the same colours as the wallpaper for fear of being in the wrong room.

And you, Madam? Women? You did say, "women?" I'd have bet a thousand to one that you'd give me that answer, which you're counting on to appear intelligent. Your case is decidedly not improving. I always knew feminism would lead women to decide to develop their brains. However, I was wrong to believe they'd all do it.

But let's continue.

Lady and Gentlemen, the only decision makers, the only ones, I want to stress, who will soon be deciding what will sell and what will not sell, are children. More precisely, boys and girls between eight and sixteen.

Look what has been going on in the past few years. Owing to the bulimic appetites of your shareholders, you have been impoverishing people. More and more ghettos are being created. "The citizen," as he has been called pretentiously, is an endangered species: tomorrow he won't be sure himself if he still exists.

This new, essentially urban animal is gradually losing all his individuality. What happens in such circumstances? We see a rise in violence, which is a new form of self-expression. For the self doesn't survive in poverty, that's well known.

Mr. President, those we consider influential and look to as opinion leaders, well, very soon they'll be children and no one else. That's right, no one but children. Which means, if you can follow me, that you'd better hold back from trying to teach them how to behave. Otherwise you won't be able to sell even a single pair of sneakers any more.

———•———

THE way to go about it is very simple. These young people gather in gangs, which are their new society, so to speak. Since ours is on the point of collapse, drained of all its values, they are creating a new one based on disillusionment. The engine of this society is power, as always, of course, but the power in this new society is based on violence in its most physical form: the purest expression of "no" to the state. The mitigating values of their parents no longer hold because they were based on the other power–purchasing power–which the parents will soon no longer have.

The children of these parents, helpless spectators of this change, are now forging a society in which they do not buy, they appropriate. So you see the gangs of thugs appear that are so poetically called "street gangs." It's back to the Wild West. The fastest draw wins, and before long no one's going to faint at the sight of a broken jaw or a pool of blood soaking into the mud.

These new young people will soon be laying down the law, and you have every reason to rejoice in it. For, providing you make the right moves, their law will make buying your shoes obligatory.

Fortunately, children have never been as manipulable as today. Since their parents have totally lost interest in their education, this is quite understandable. I have not had children, and I confess to sympathy for the parents. I recall making a little calculation of what a child costs his parents. In money, of course, but also in time. The result completely turned me off having any. Having a child means amputating half one's life for fifteen years. Look at the animal world. What other species spends fifteen years of its life wiping its offspring clean? It doesn't make sense. You really have to believe you're immortal to let yourself lose fifteen years of your life that way. Often the best years, too. So the disaffection we see these days is altogether natural. The result is that children are left to their own devices at an age closer and closer to their birth. They're conceived, brought into the world, given their bottles, then suddenly they're getting the message that their lives are their own and shouldn't be taking away from ours. While some of them adjust quickly to this early independence, most keep searching for identification with something that can give them a degree of stability.

"The gang," a sense of belonging, plays a vital role, Mr. President, and it is precisely with this that you must gather them up and make them yours. You'll do them a service by gathering them, besides. For these still fragile young people, it will be like a homecoming. Their gratitude will be great, which of course will deepen their attachment to your cause and thereby their loyalty. You must understand how to take advantage of their pressing need for self-assertion. Left alone at an earlier and earlier age, they have an increasingly precocious and pronounced need to strike back with self-assertion. By leaving them to themselves, their parents invite them to take their places. It's a well-known phenomenon: deny me and I'll assert myself with a vengeance.

Their self-assertion inevitably passes through a certain form of brutality. Someone who is rejected seeks to impose himself by any means available. The result is that these little monsters become kings of the house, the street, and the entire city. They are the ones who make the decisions, in the name of the independence that has just been thrust on them.

You too must surely know families whose children were never allowed to. Never allowed to do what? To do anything. At ten they're not playing yet so they won't get dirty. At fifteen they still have to have their shoelaces tied. At twenty they wait for their mothers to get up and make their breakfast. At thirty they're still living at home. There are less and less of these families, but there are still some, to show by contrast the family of today whose eight-year-old child makes his own breakfast in a house that the parents have already left for their workplaces, or to which they've not yet come home after a night out. After breakfast this child should put on your company's shoes, Mr. President. Not just any shoes, but ones he has chosen himself. Why? To assert his own existence. Because he does and must exist.

These children, Mr. President, will be the key to your success.

I estimate the cost of the operation at about a third of your present marketing budget. If you find this too much (for I know your shareholders are asking for new rounds of cost-cutting), I shall pack up and go back to Greece by the three o'clock plane without even submitting my account. I'm foresighted by habit: I've booked a window seat. That way I'll be able to see the waves that will carry you off.

You'll allow me to continue? I'm delighted. From your curiosity may come wisdom.

The first step will be to infiltrate all the small gangs in all the Western world's cities of more than five million inhabitants. Every city of that size has several active gangs, so count on finding around seven thousand.

These young people lay down the law in their neighbourhoods. If they decide, in an arbitrary way essentially, to go after anyone who rollerblades or wears striped pants, you would be well advised not to go rollerblading or wear striped pants because without a word of warning they will descend on you in a horde and put you straight. These clans are veritable little mafias, Mr. President, and neither your millions nor your renown will stop them from tearing off your rollerblades and stuffing the roller wheels one by one you-know-where. Perhaps even two by two if that amuses them.

You'll give these young people armed with sticks, knives, sometimes even handguns, a mission to impose a new law. A very simple law: all the young must wear disposable shoes so as to turn their progenitors' consumer reflexes to ridicule. You'll pay them so their gangs will attack other young people first, then older ones, and confiscate their shoes. They'll cut those shoes up into pieces and leave them on the sidewalks to show very clearly that they're no longer acceptable, that life is being reinvented, and disposables are what people will wear from now on.

The first months of the operation will benefit you greatly because you will sell off all your inventories of old, durable shoes. The victims will have to replace what they lose. At first they won't realize that they'll have the new ones torn off their feet again a few days after buying them.

You want to leave us, Madam? I understand. The strategy I'm explaining at the moment is rather disturbing. I agree. However, you'll forgive me for having insisted with your chief that the door to this room be locked. You understand that any leakage of information would be prejudicial to the company that pays you. Far too well, I might say, but that's a strictly personal opinion. No, no, don't worry, your freedom will be restored in a few hours. You're only sequestered for the duration of this meeting. Your chief will then explain your choices, with whose generosity you can have no cause for complaint. My most faithful assistants were never treated with as much consideration, whereas they had talent.

You're not going to ask these thugs to beat people up wholesale, Mr. President. It just means using the terror they're already spreading to channel their efforts so as to speed the change in people's thinking. They're going to love it; their obsession's going to seem so surrealistic. Imagine the scene for a minute. Your little angels are walking along the street with their little friends. At the corner, a gang of these law enforcers challenge them and with a smirk tell them to take off their godawful shoes and beat it, or else spend a very nasty quarter hour. The angels quake in their boots, take them off, run home, and hide under their mothers' skirts. What's happened? Nothing. They haven't even been beaten up. They've been obliged, strongly obliged, to leave their shoes on the spot because they're old-fashioned. Because they're no longer wearable. Because people nowadays wear only disposable shoes and you're not allowed to walk around in anything else. The next morning their mothers will go to one of your stores in a very cranky mood and buy a pair of shoes for which they will pay a bit less this time. Since you never know.

A week later, the same story. The little darlings come home barefoot again, though, it must be said, less terrorized this time. Their mothers are twice as much. They're all upset, but not for long because the solution to the problem comes straight from the mouths of the cunningly converted little dinkums: their mothers must buy disposable shoes. Quite simply because, as the gangs said clearly, from now on everybody wears disposable shoes. Those and no others, little friends.

You'll have guessed the sequel, of course. Since young people decide what one wears and what one doesn't wear, the directive spreads to the populace in general at the hallucinatory speed of a trail of snow. To be young, to belong to one's time, but really because we're made to, we'll all wear disposable shoes.

You have children, Madam? Yes? I'm reassured. You do serve a purpose, then. So confirm this for me. First, that your child has not been mistreated in this story. Not in the least. Second, that your next purchase will be a pair of disposable shoes for which you will pay far less and which will protect your poor little lambkin from that gang of thugs. Isn't it true? There. I knew you'd be more reasonable when you'd heard my case. The trouble with you, Madam, is that you don't listen. You form your opinions on the basis of what you think I'm going to say instead of waiting respectfully to know my point of view. One can see that you're used to giving orders. But we'll leave that: I'm not under contract to conduct your trial.

Allow me, Lady and Gentlemen, to add to my case an observation that is sure to appeal to you and those of your shareholders who are obsessed with market share. My observation is this: from the minute disposable shoes become the norm and my gangsterist strategy has begun to bear fruit, your competitors' shares will begin to fall in value as you'd never dared hope. Developing disposable shoes, which is to say, designing them and converting your production facilities, will take you several months. Those several months will suffice amply to let you occupy the whole of the market without having the competition underfoot. Their reaction time will be too long for them to survive your headstart. Sales of durable shoes will last no longer than two months, after which they'll be reduced to zero. My strategy, Mr. President, will give your company a consummate monopoly in footwear. This alone is worth all the gold in the world. My bill will not neglect this consideration.

Although this strategy is already faultless, I shall add a recommendation worthy of the most exceptional strategists, of whom I am one. I recommend that you give, rather than sell, the universal soles I was talking about minutes ago.

If I were in the oil industry, I would give cars to anyone who signed on to have them repaired at my garages and to buy my oil and gasoline. Believe me, while looking like the Good Samaritan, I'd make a fortune. If you give the sole the upper is attached to, and the upper only costs $3, no company will be able to compete with you and you'll have the whole market to yourselves in less time than you'll need to realize what's just happened.

Pardon me? You have a question, Sir? Please, go ahead. I know I talk a lot, but unlike the lady, I can also listen. You'll understand, though, that after three months almost alone on that Greek island I was telling you about, it's nice to have an audience. Solitude is a treasure beyond compare, but I confess being a bit bored at times having only myself to talk to. Although I always have something interesting to tell myself.

Your question, Sir?

I can see your anxiety. I don't share it, though. And to answer your question, allow me to return to that marvellous island from where I was able to cast an eye at our civilization. The film of History that I saw over and over in my mind's eye taught me many things about human behaviour patterns. I already understood these behaviour patterns from having spent my life studying them, and even influencing them. But several little things had escaped me, and that island isolation placed them in full light for me.

Cast an eye on the past with me and wonder, I urge you, why men have always so easily allowed others, who most often have been very weak and unstable, to impose themselves on their kind. History is full of examples of peoples who woke up one morning under the heel of a dictator who had given them plenty of warning and whose only strength was to have decided that he would be the strongest. Even though in fact he was nothing of the kind, and was small and absurd compared with the number of individuals who, that day, decided not to resist his will for power.

The truth, Sir, is that power belongs not to the greater number but to the greater will. And if the greater will overcomes the greater number, time after time, it's because the victims do not resolve to prevent it. Will uses unconventional weapons and thumbs its nose at laws and conventions. Those who would oppose it, to the contrary, use only conventional weapons and with respect for laws and conventions, pretending that their behaviour should be more civilized and legitimate than the aggressor's. The result is that the aggressor can advance without any real resistance.

So no, Sir, no one's going to make serious efforts to put a stop to this sponsored activity. Especially since its violence will be much more verbal than physical. I even predict that groups not sponsored by your company will imitate those you have trained, entranced by this operation in which they recognize the nonconformity and derision they consider to be their own since they dropped out of present-day society. The one that no longer offers them anything. Not a thing. Furthermore, the fact that the weapon used will be unconventional and the damage done relatively harmless compared with the kicks and beatings usually delivered will have this activity even finding approval among a good many of the people we were speaking about earlier, those whose self-respect you are currently destroying with great slashings of their incomes. They will cheer to see these heroic troops unwittingly promoting cheap, supposedly recyclable shoes, whose manufacturer they will liken to a new Robin Hood unobsessed with profits. An idea that you will cultivate yourselves with great lashings of public relations.

You're afraid of the police? Come, now. Where's the real threat from these shoe-stealing clowns who do no physical harm to their victims? The police have other fish to fry. Today, at this very moment, squadrons of people are replying on help lines to wives beaten by their husbands, restaurant managers who find corpses in their washrooms, small-time drug dealers who can't shake off the system, bar owners coping with drunkards smashing up the joint, young boys victimized by false priests and real pedophiles, etc. So what do you think the lady on the phone at the police station will say to the lady in tears who tells her her son has had his sneakers lifted, eh? No, Sir, there's not much chivalry in the operation, I grant you. But what congenial entertainment compared with all the real physical violence our citizens are victims of at present!

The second point you raised, Sir, is far more serious. But rest assured, I have foreseen the matter. You're entirely right. It could never be a question of really paying these young leaders to put their followers to work advancing your plans. When I talk about paying them, I don't mean remunerating them but giving them importance, which will cost you far less, will be perfectly legal, less dangerous, and much more effective. You're not going to turn these young people into employees, but scouts. This is exactly what they need more than anything, since most of them already have enough money for their meagre requirements. The manner in which they appropriate money is not the most honourable, but never mind. We can't help that. What we must understand, what concerns us, is that they don't need our cash. Importance is what they're after, and don't have. The proof is that they make themselves important through terror. They wield terror altogether gratuitously and with no objective other than to demonstrate their existence to their victims. Therefore, give them an existence and suddenly they'll become as effective as a whole battalion and without asking a penny of compensation. All you need do is supply the pretext, so to speak, plus the disposables, and they'll march in the direction you'll have indicated.

I have very often been asked to create trends in years gone by. Strange as it may seem, nothing is simpler than launching a trend, even without much investment. Find people who have nothing, give them something, tell them this something makes them somebody, and presto, your job's done. They're so proud to be somebody, they think they're unique, powerful, superior. They say it, live it, show it, and presto, your trend is launched.

This is what you do already, at high prices, however, when you launch a new style of shoes. You call it "market skimming." The difference is that these people (who have nothing) to whom you're giving something are those who have money. You take advantage of the fact they have money to relieve them of it. To make quite sure they buy, furthermore, you sell them your innovations at three times the price of the shoes they already have on their feet. Owning those shoes will certainly make them somebody! So they buy them, show them, parade around in them all over the city, and that's the way they launch your new style. It's child's play.

I know several of you will be repelled by the thought of implementing this strategy that's at odds with what you've learned from your marketing textbooks. But something we must be sure we understand is this: it's much less a matter of launching a product than of channeling behaviour patterns toward reflexes that will serve your ends. If you believe that implementing outworn strategies will maintain your growth, you will not achieve your ends. Your company today has arrived at a stage in its evolution that requires you to think differently and act resolutely. Any hesitation will place your future on a declining path. You must forge ahead, banishing from your thoughts the idea that you can win without cheating. Marketing theorists are soon going to be recycling themselves as ice-cream vendors. I predict it with the assurance of the one who knows them from having trained them.

What a funny face you're making, Mr. President. I read in your eyes that you're wondering if I'm serious at the moment. You're imagining, on your way home at the end of your working day, seeing a band of leather-clad youths in the process of making some honest little boys in your neighbourhood remove their shoes. You're decidedly not amused. You'd even be tempted to tell yourself that that's hardly an honest way to earn a living.

If that's what you're thinking at the moment, Mr. President, you should explain something to me: how can you go to sleep at night knowing that children ten years old work twelve hours a day to earn a few cents sewing the shoes you sell?

Don't reply. I'd rather shut my eyes too. What money would you pay my fees with if you didn't make profits? I only want to point out to you that my sales strategy is much less disturbing than your manufacturing strategy. And before questioning the legality of my strategy, you must question the legitimacy of yours.

Let's continue.

How much time will be needed for this operation to take effect? I can't tell you precisely; it will all depend on how much effort you're willing to put into it. I'll make a prediction, however: not much time. I base this on my observation of today's youth. Young people adopt styles with startling alacrity. We in this room belong to a generation so attached to its old values that corporations had a terrible time getting us to accept change. The young of today are quite the opposite. They buy what's new even before it comes on the market. They never get enough of it, and for them even the most durable products are disposable. Including their parents, whom they look on as products too.

In the days when adults were the biggest consumers, thinking durable was the guide for our corporations. Soon, when adults have spent what remains of their excess money (once the source of all their power), choices will be dictated by young people. Not with money, but with the violence of their rebellion against all durable possessions. Trust my intuition: to them, durable possessions will symbolize defeat, the unattainability of the buying power their parents had, and therefore the loss of their identity. Hence the importance for you of adopting my strategy without delay and figuring among the major suppliers of the tools of rebellion. Whether you like it or not, the young will strike soon. Let's have them do it with weapons bought from you!

That should answer your worries, Sir. We can now move along to the following point, which I shall call the crucial phase of the strategy that will make your company the foremost of a new era.

But I can hear your stomachs growling. Perhaps it would be wiser if we ate your finger food before we tackle this new phase. I'm feeling a little peckish myself.

WHAT'S on that bread? *Pâté de campagne*, country pâté? Yes, please. With a little water, yes. Thank you. I'm making your mouths water, and here I am, feeling dry myself.

In Greece, I took to eating very lightly at midday. I have to say that stuffing oneself in that heat isn't recommended. It's better to wait for evening, when a cool little breeze rises and liberates you from the oppressive heat of daytime.

Do I go swimming? No, not much. I spend the better part of my days sitting in the shade of a tree, looking out at the sea, watching the waves and the birds. It's very restful, you know, letting oneself be lulled like that. Early in the morning, before the sun pins me to my chair, I go and take my turn polishing the stones of temples raised by people long ago to the glory of the gods of their time. It's very moving to think that our feet are walking the same stones trodden by men and women over 2,500 years ago! The very same stones! You stand on a stone and you say to yourself: on this very spot a man was standing 2,500 years ago, wearing a kind of toga and pondering the meaning of life. Then you'll turn your thoughts to the future and you'll wonder whether, in another 2,500 years, there will still be humans on Earth who will come and visit this place again. And will think of us, perhaps, men of the twenty-first century, who came here to ponder the meaning of ... shoes.

Could you tell me what is the most noteworthy resemblance between ancient Greece and our modern world? In my opinion it's our common conviction, unadmitted but nevertheless very deeply held, that there are demigods among us. I have visited amphitheatres where in ancient times performances were given in which actors played the parts of men recognized by Olympus as demigods. It has been said that, during these performances, the spectators became agitated and entered a kind of trance. Isn't that what still happens today when rock groups blast out their amplified megawatts to audiences of 100,000? On stage, those are demigods bursting our eardrums. And their music is the religion of the century.

Forgive my indiscretion, Sir, but may I ask what that is that you're drinking? Ah, yes. An energy drink. That confirms what I was just saying. We are all more or less convinced that we have demigods among us; even more, that we are among them. This drink is a truly divine invention. Short of giving you strength, it gives you the illusion of it. Just as the fact that all of us being together on the … what floor are we on here? … I forget. Thirty-second. Thank you. The mere fact of being higher than others already places us in a superior social position. We're halfway between men and the gods. We look at things from on high. Gives you a nice vertigo. Don't you have the impression, as I do myself, that you're demi-gods? Of course, modesty keeps you from being honest.

But tell me a little about your daughter, Mr. President. Has she finished at the Conservatory? Yes? Congratulations. And what has she been doing since? She's teaching music? At the Conservatory, I presume. To other young ladies who in years to come will teach at the Conservatory. It was foreseeable. It's called going nowhere. I don't say that to be unpleasant, believe me. It's even rather out of jealousy: I have never been able to resign myself to doing something non-productive. Like my grandfather, who was a man of the theatre. When I was small, I kept asking him why he was always pretending rather than doing things for real.

I learned a lot in the wings of the theatre. That was my first business school, to tell the truth. It was there I found out that people are very docile, very malleable, and readily go along with being what one wants them to be. All you need do is give them the right costume, makeup, and cue. They even do so well they enjoy it. From indolence, no doubt. It's so much easier to do what we're told to do.

My father? He was a lawyer for a reinsurance firm, one of those companies that insures the insurers. Our society must have become very complex and very insecure when even insurance companies don't feel assured without being insured themselves. And yet no investment is sure any more. These people sell insecurity, but they don't ever buy it.

One day, my father showed me just how complex our law has become. It's really fascinating, you know. Its structure makes one think of the streets in our old city centres. We've patched them over so many times instead of repairing them properly, we must have raised our cities by several metres, isn't that so? It was easier and faster to plug the holes, so that's what we did. Today's laws have been built up in the same way. To the very first laws, we have added amendment after amendment to make those laws evolve along with society. We have patched them over. This is how lawyers have gradually created a world in which they've become indispensable.

One of you is a software expert, I believe. That's you? You'll confirm, I'm sure, that a great deal of present-day software is like our roads. To original versions, we have added instructions to replace this or that function by another. We're in the patching-over period. The trouble is, it all gets pretty cumbersome. Imagine the weight of a jacket patched twenty times over.

Tell me, Mr. President, have you settled your dispute with the unions? You were at the negotiation stage this winter, were you not? How long did the strike last finally? Two months? That's not long. But you have to understand the unions' point of view. Since they've been investing in corporations, it's much harder for them to slow down production. Not considering that the more they get, the less their shares return. The mutual fund is a brilliant invention. Co-operative management too. Replacing wages by dividends leads to marvellous savings.

Pardon me? Oh, you're asking me a very difficult question. I think I'd put my money on arms manufacturers. No, I'm not a warmonger, but I can count. How many of us are there on this Earth? That's what we need to know. Between you and me, Hitler wasn't so crazy. Take Africa. Living space is beginning to run short for many native Africans, that's clear. As for the Chinese, it's only a matter of time before they begin shooting at each other. Why do you think they've been persecuting Tibet unless it's to put off their own blow-up? The Chinese could count long before we could, you know. Since their number has become a missile, I'd be inclined to invest in launchers.

You invest in works of art? You like taking risks. Those works that you tell me are immortal are dead and gone, believe me. A few years from now, paintings will be reproduced in such quantities that they won't be worth any more than the frames around them. It will soon be impossible to tell the real from the false, technology is progressing so fast. I'd be upset by this if I could appreciate fine art, but I confess I don't know a thing about it. That a single brush stroke could be worth a million others is something that is completely beyond me.

And you, Sir? In the technologies? You're right. But you have to know which. I have a friend who is a passionate devotee of artificial intelligence. He has single-handedly financed a company that does highly specialized research in the subject. Their work is very advanced, too. The proof is that every time they put a question to their machine it produces a dozen different answers, some of them sometimes even contradicting the others. It's definitely very close to the human brain.

Thank you, no, I won't have any more. That country pâté isn't bad, but since there's less and less country nowadays, what we're left with, so to speak, is the pâté. I have to watch the state of my liver.

WHERE were we? Yes, that was it. At the second phase of my action plan. Thank you for reminding me.

Pardon me? I confess I was expecting that. Yes, it's true. I think I really roused your curiosity minutes ago by not giving away all of my thinking all at once. No, it wasn't a put-on. It's just that the moment wasn't right. But it is true, yes, that having grown up with the theatre, I learned not to tell everything in the first five minutes of a presentation. You have to be able to hold your audience.

Very well. Agreed. So before continuing, I will tell you what will happen if you let things drift. I know you won't believe me. Why? Quite simply because you would much rather not believe me. How many people seriously consider what they don't want to see? If I'm one of that élite group that do, don't think it's just masochism on my part. It's because it's my duty, by vocation, always to take account of all sides of a question. Even the sides I'd rather not see. That's how I come to a better understanding of our society at all levels and others will never, ever make it.

Here goes anyway. Whether you believe me or not detracts nothing from the gravity of my assertions. In the worst case, you'll conclude that I'm more artist than strategist, and in fifteen years you'll say that in the final analysis I was more strategist than artist. I'll only be ahead of you in my grave.

I told you that the effect of deciding not to make the change I'm prescribing would be a steep decline ten or at the very most fifteen years from now. You want to know how, and I'm about to tell you.

No Sir.

At this moment there is a growing number of individuals dreaming of reinventing the world. This is not new. There have always been people ready to play hero and attempt to overthrow the established order. In the days of kings, they wanted to guillotine the monarchy. In colonial times, they wanted to re-establish countries for indigenous peoples. Today they're turning on the multinationals because they know it's you who are in control. You are their new battlefield. If they have a chance to go down in History, which is essential to their motivation, it will be by overturning you, since at present you are the strongest.

While there are more of these rebels wanting to overturn you than in previous centuries, it's not because you're more monstrous than the monarchs of the past.

Quite the contrary; they'd have trouble convincing us that they're slaves in need of liberation. They're white-shoe rebels. Their number is accounted for essentially by demographic growth, coupled with the fact that we have had the munificence to educate them. Democratization of education, then of the press, has surely played against us. That's what we've got for our generosity.

In what way could they overturn you, in your opinion? For all their growing numbers, and although their arguments are sometimes defensible, it certainly won't be by mobilizing populations at large. Because while our institutions were educating these rebels, our marketing strategies were winning over most, composed—fortunately—of the loyal consumers who wouldn't for the world risk losing their privileges. Everybody wants to see a better world, as long as everybody can keep going to the movies and out for a bite to eat. So there won't be any social mobilization; no Western population is going to go down into the streets in sufficient numbers to ask the multinationals to cut back on their marketing ambitions. That would be judged lethal for its treasured comforts that are already seriously compromised.

No, Mr. President, these people are preparing to foil your ambitions and momentum with a far more malevolent strategy. My prediction is that tomorrow they'll create small-scale cottage-industry companies and the day after they'll gather them together in a kind of federation. And after that do you know what they'll do? They'll launch an all-out battle against you, on your own turf, using your own strategies. They too will manufacture desirable shoes, hiring gifted designers, and they'll market them with advice from strategists just as clever as the one before you now. They'll offer irresistible shoes with a diabolical sales pitch: that, plain to see, their products are handmade and their sales support local craftspeople. Which will be true since they'll all have sworn not to take profits. It's not hard to figure. Take your salary and your executives' salaries, add hidden fringe benefits and compensations (which often amount to more than your total salaries), add rental values on your sumptuous offices, add your benefits of all kinds, natures, and sources, declared and undeclared (which are pretty expensive to maintain), and you'll realize why you'll be in no position to compete with them. The single fact of having shareholders disqualifies you from competing because your competition will be most cleverly protected from these grasping creatures by financing their growth in other ways. Probably through co-operatives.

These people who want your hide are not organized at the moment. As I've already said, they're content just parading in the streets with their banners, banging on their pots. But soon, very soon, they'll be setting up little businesses, and someone, somewhere, will give them the idea of getting together. That day won't be very far off, and will be the beginning of the end for you. And you won't have the slightest chance of reacting to your own advantage.

I know it's more comfortable to think that this is all just the fruit of my imagination. It's so much pleasanter to believe that the protesters of our time are happy in their role as small-time agitators and take enough satisfaction from playing prophets in the society that created them. But if you open your eyes a little wider you'll find it very hard not to see that there are more and more of them and they're more vocal all the time. There are not many protest movements, but they're more active than you think. In conjunction with each of the major meetings you organize with your kind, they exchange ideas in ways that take advantage of the visibility given them by the press on these occasions. More locally, they organize into small cells that are always ready to interfere with your business activities. These pressure groups increase in number every year and, while it's not uncommon to see some appear that are merely frivolous, to us they are symptomatic of the growing will of these people to organize, if only to talk to someone who shares their ideas–at least their rejection of the ideas of others.

All revolutions begin this way, with the massing of groups of people saying, "no." At first they don't really know what they're saying "no" to. Then there comes a day when someone whispers an answer to the question. However little the answer gets through, this massing becomes dangerous to a point we cannot continue to ignore. It would be possible to undermine the arguments of these people if their audience had a few grams of grey matter, but that is not the case. Every David who battles Goliath very easily wins plenty of sympathy. Especially if the Davids are clever and take care never to say that what they want is not to kill Goliath but replace him.

That, Mr. President, is why I'm telling you that my strategy is not just brilliant but indispensable.

———•———

THE first phase, to recapitulate, consisted of making footwear a perishable product and getting it worn through a rather unconventional strategy, but one capable of guaranteeing rapid achievement of your goal.

The second phase will enable you to establish your supremacy to the point where the grandchildren of your grandchildren can live in the greatest comfort. If civilization still exists, of course.

How will you ensure that you will continue to dominate this budding century and keep a perpetual grasp on consumers? Gradually, Mr. President, you will impose a tax that will give recognition of acceptance. I told you when I came into this room that the action plan I would propose, the one you asked me for, would be more Machiavellian than anything all of you here could have dreamed up together. And I hasten to reassure you, my dear Madam, that you and your descendants will follow it gladly and without any strong-arm coercion.

Since you and those like you, and I'm speaking here of other corporations of your size, are all working toward the desirable disappearance of what we have called the middle class, it must be agreed that governments will very soon no longer have enough revenues to provide the services considered necessary by those who still define themselves as citizens. These services once considered essential and right for advanced societies are already near extinction. I was talking minutes ago about roads being patched over, but that's only one of the manifestations (a very visible one, granted) that are awaiting the people. Very soon it's going to be the people themselves whom we'll be patching over in the hospitals. They won't come out cured but with temporary relief, mostly just drugged with analgesics, or even anaesthetics. As for teaching institutions, they will change vocation gradually with the disappearance of thought.

I'm not prophesying some future natural catastrophe, nuclear clearout, or military dictatorship. I'm talking frankly about the society toward which we are moving as efficaciously as possible, in which a few large companies like yours will have succeeded where others have failed. The society born of the economic concentration that you cultivate, and that will soon have left in shreds all the so-called social gains of recent decades.

I haven't spoken of hospitals and teaching institutions by chance, of course. Together, they gobble up most of all the budgets still managed by the State.

In order to master the future and make the people manageable, you will have to learn to govern by taking the example of the most reasonable nations on the subject, those that work for you at present. These nations, if we can still talk about nations, are run by people who have learned not to care for the health of their people and even less to educate them. Why? To keep them from thinking, Mr. President. These régimes use arms, which is very ugly, but you have to agree that they very easily achieve their ends. We have the intelligence to behave otherwise because we pretend to be civilized, but we will achieve the same objectives.

Operating rooms and classrooms, we were saying, together take up the lion's share of budgets still available to States. In a way this is excellent because as soon as citizens cease to have enough income to pay income tax, which is beginning to happen, most of these will be closed. All that will be left will be private institutions where, for rich people like you and me, it will be possible to obtain real services. Health and education will again be what they should have stayed: not rights but privileges.

You'll forgive me for being brutal, but it's important to consider that the duty of societies is not to care for their people's health and educate them, it's to give them the illusion of being in good health and educated. Which is not the same thing at all.

The most successful businesses of our age must be taken as examples. What do these big companies (including yours) sell today? Products? No. They sell illusion. It's plain to see in every field where sales amount to billions of dollars. You can be sure that you absolutely have to create an illusion that can be shared if you're going to sell that many products to that many people of cultures that are often very different. And you have to sell the illusions you create instead of continuing to try to sell products.

Have you been to the beach recently? You should go. It's very instructive. You'll see loads of people identical in every way. They all have the same bathing suits that they've seen advertised on TV. They're all wearing the same sunglasses. They're all reading the latest issue of the same magazine. The children are all playing with the same beach toy of the year, and everybody is smelling of the same suntan lotion that will give everyone the same golden glow. Why? Because people have been told how to behave at the beach. They've been told to be the same. That's why.

The same thing should be repeated about health and education. What is important, you see, is to create the right expectations and then satisfy them. Our governments have functioned the other way round for too long. They have bolstered the worship of health care and learning and then ruined themselves trying to keep their promises. These objects of worship must be dismantled. We must stop propagating all those statistics on life expectancy and percentages of university grads in our populations. We must stop praising good physical and mental condition. No one will mind because people are tired of playing tennis and studying. They do it because they must or should, or just because they're told it's a good thing to do. When we've stopped praising it, I guarantee they'll stop making each other sweat. They'll go to the beach with their precious sunglasses, cover each other with their suntan lotion, and plant their bums in the sand holding the magazine of the month. Not a magazine to read; a magazine to look at. And they'll be happy as clams to stay there and not move.

A new conception of health care and education will have to be developed and then applied. A conception based not on performance but on fashion and conformity.

Standards will have to be lowered. Can everyone afford a house in the country and a private aeroplane? No. Then why should everyone be in perfect health and smothered in university degrees? Our society can't afford that any more. People will have to be made to understand that. Better still, they'll have to be told how to understand the new concepts of health care and education. Health care should be limited to relief of pain and education should consist of knowing enough to read our advertising slogans. Nothing more. Anything beyond these definitions is a luxury that no one can afford to pay for anymore. People might as well be prepared at once to think differently.

Pardon me? Yes, you're right. That small Greek island did indeed help sharpen my thinking. Do you believe the people who lived there 2,500 years ago died at the age of ninety because they jumped around with stones? Do you believe they could all read and write? Were they less happy? Over the centuries, we've not only created élitist definitions of health care and education but we've spread the idea–which is really inexcusable–that everyone should belong to the élite. If that isn't getting ourselves in a heap of shit, I wonder what is!

I was saying a minute ago that people would be delighted with this downgrading of present standards in health care and education. It's not an exaggeration. The process has already begun; all that's needed is to strengthen it and speed up its implementation.

Yes, Sir. It has already begun. Young people have been leaving school for several years to go in for activities that regularly put their lives in danger. The illusion merchants we were talking about have less and less trouble selling them the idea of living now and as intensely as possible. These new lifestyles don't square very well with the thought of leaving university at thirty and dying at 120. Let's say rather that the young drive at 120 and die at thirty.

That said, if health care consists of not being in pain, analgesics still must be paid for. And if education consists of learning to read, we have to be taught. All this means that governments will need to have a few shekels, which they soon won't have any more because they won't be collecting enough income tax.

Who's going to pay? You, Mr. President. Yes, you.

What a strange feeling I'm reading on your faces. Is it skepticism or worry? I can't tell. If it's worry I shall reassure you at once that, no, I'm not going to recommend either that you open hospitals or that you open schools. Even less buy them. The terms of my contract don't include running up expenses for you. Apart from my fee, of course.

No, I'm going to talk to you about a much more profitable strategy. And I'll begin by putting a new question to you: what real role should government play in this age when you, big business, pull all the economic strings? There isn't an easy answer. In the days of monarchies, the role of government was to steal the wealth of peasants. Once the monarchies had fallen, it was decided that its role should be to divide up that wealth. Theoretically, of course, because in fact we simply replaced monarchs with corporations, leaving government a few crumbs to scatter here and there. But now that there's no wealth left at all, because everything's concentrated in corporate hands, what indeed is the role of government?

To redistribute poverty? That's the peak of cynicism as an answer. No. The role of government today is to pretend. You ought to know since you're the ones who put it in place and dictate its policies.

Governments today pretend to govern because you've taken away all their powers. You've treated them as you have your employees; today they're helpless, penniless, and obedient to your will. Their power of intervention is slimmer and slimmer, with the result that health care and education are the only real jurisdictions left to them. Everything else is under your rule.

Why have you still not wrestled the health care and education budgets away from governments? Because you have scruples, Mr. President. As I've already said, the plan I'm proposing has none. You're paying me to turn scruples into profits.

Even if you insist on letting the State handle these things, in a few years it will no longer be able to. You will have reduced people's incomes so drastically that no one will be paying enough income tax to feed its meagre coffers. You will actively enter the scene at this moment. The State can no longer provide your health care? The State can no longer educate you? We will do it instead. Your government has betrayed you, abandoned you, bled you dry? Not to worry. We're really generous, we'll pay the bill.

This prospect is the brainchild of pure genius, Mr. President. Just picture it: when incomes drop, you reduce the price of shoes; when health-care budgets dwindle, you pay the bills. Can't you see yourself as the most popular CEO in the country? You're going to give people what even their political leaders, who were democratically elected to serve them, can no longer provide.

Health care will cost you something, to be sure, but education will cost almost nothing because it will be quite enough for people just to learn how to read. To those who distinguish themselves, you will give more advanced training according to the needs of your company.

But I can see that again you're letting yourselves fall prey to skepticism, even disbelief. I'm a bit troubled by that. Though rather flattered at the same time because you're showing me proof of my superiority. Since it does seem once more that I have the monopoly on clairvoyance, let's look at some details of this strategy.

Believe me, everything will happen with no fuss whatever. And without violence, Madam. I know you're sensitive about these things: it goes with weakness and insecurity.

———•———

YOU will see that the strategy I have developed is astonishingly clever. It will be far more profitable, besides, than the plan I presume is being put forward by all those harebrained companies that are trying to convince governments to privatize health-care and educational services.

You know several of these companies, Mr. President. You know their ambitions as well as how they expect to reach their goals. They want governments to hand over management of these services to them. Hypocritically, they promise to maintain both their quality and universal access to them. They want private powers to replace public powers. I would like to challenge their accountants. It would give me pleasure to expose one of the following: either they're hiding their real intentions, or they can't count.

When I withdrew to my island, the only equipment I took with me for my work was my cellphone. The statement of my calls and their cost is attached to my bill. I'm warning you now, it's a hefty sum. Though everything's relative: I was able to confirm my hypotheses with these calls, and prepare the ground for your second offensive.

What you are going to do in footwear, other companies will inevitably do in other fields. Not immediately because not many of them are as fortunate as you in having a particularly gifted consultant. But it's only a question of time before these companies capture the better part of their respective markets through strategies whose sole and urgent purpose, like yours, is to get back their own consumers before they disappear.

The important thing, you see, will be to get ahead of these companies and make yourselves the gateway to the protection and increase of market share for any company wanting to grow rather than perish.

I'll explain because it's clear you don't understand at all.

In the near future you will have become the only company in the footwear sector worthy of the name, with a clientele emotionally wedded to your products. On the strength of this position, Mr. President, you must prepare a proposal that simply cannot be turned down by any company that wants to live rather than die. A double proposal, I should say, the first addressed to the companies and the second to their customers.

From Greece, I communicated with several companies of relatively the same size as yours. I talked at length with their presidents. I never talk to vice-presidents, much less executive officers. They're either intelligent but have no power, or they have power but aren't intelligent. It's one of the weaknesses of our administrative structures. Something we've inherited from public structures. Big business has always revelled in putting on governmental airs.

Just imagine–this is only a parenthetical by-the-way–one of these presidents was mere kilometres away from me, on vacation in Greece with his entourage aboard his modest little yacht.

I told them all, without mentioning your name, that we were on the point of offering them exactly what they were looking for. As I expected, they all began by replying politely that they weren't looking for anything and therefore my offer–whatever it was–was of no interest to their company.

Of all possible replies, they all chose the only stupid one. Would you believe me if I told you that all the presidents of fifteen of the most tentacular corporations, one after the other, admitted to me by phone that they didn't know what problem they're facing? It's true. All these people are working at something other than ensuring their future; they don't even know there's danger awaiting them. Consider yourselves privileged, Lady and Gentlemen. Your President, here facing me, is probably the only one of his rank to have foreseen the danger and commissioned a strategist to escape catastrophe. Mr. President, I hereupon pay you a tribute that you deserve.

Since I had anticipated their reply, I had of course prepared the follow-up. All I had to do was paint a picture in a few words of the present and the future, and they were begging me to call them back the instant this proposal was ready for presentation.

What if I told you, Mr. President, that I represent an already huge company that tomorrow is going to have a monopoly in an essential consumer product. What if I told you that the day after tomorrow this company will have installed an infallible technique for keeping the loyalty of its customers despite all the parades and speeches of all those environmentalist troublemakers and self-styled precursors of a new anti-multinational world order? What if I told you that the day after that, the same company will have put together a conglomerate of complementary companies that will jointly maintain consumption by those customers and guarantee the company's growth without reviving the middle class? Wouldn't you row your boat back to port to be very sure not to miss my visit? Those presidents are waiting with a hand on the telephone. In a word, they're slavering.

The thing's very simple for all that. It's a two-stage plan.

First, we must continue to weaken governments to make it financially impossible for them to give health-care and educational services to their populations. We're not far from that critical point, but we must act quickly to be ahead of those clowns we were talking about earlier, who are better at greasing political palms to get what they want than working at solid financial planning.

The fastest way to stymie governments is with the strategy used by practitioners of commercial law. To win a case even when they're wrong, they block the wheels of justice to exhaust their opponent. They use laws and jurisprudence, obviously, but also rules of procedure in order to drag out a trial interminably. The plaintiff spends all his energy and all his money just manoeuvring to keep the case going. Exhaustion eventually leads him to give up: he can no longer proceed, with the proceedings or otherwise.

This is a kind of technical knockout, and in my opinion it's the example to follow. To finish off democracy without bearing the blame and disapproval for the oper-ation in the eyes of the people, we have to get the governments peppered with lawsuits. Tens of thousands of individual but simultaneous lawsuits instituted by ordinary citizens in the wake of detrimental experiences attributable to the State's health-care services, claiming compensations totaling several hundreds of billions of dollars. The cases don't need to be winning ones. What is important is to force trials and oblige the governments to defend themselves. You'll agree that the big winners in this legal saga will be the lawyers on both sides, which will have them in our pockets from square one for getting these multiple trials on the rails. To keep their wives and mistresses happy, it's entirely in their interests if the parties don't see eye to eye. So with consummate pleasure, they'll make things last.

Governments already badly hurt by increasing costs in their health-care systems will need both to pay legal costs and increase their hospital budgets to prevent new lawsuits. They'll very quickly have their hands full and no longer be able to find enough financing to put out all those fires. They'll be in a budgetary squeeze, but even more they'll be in a social squeeze. For at the palace gates, there will be more pot-bangers than ever, ringing their knell. Health care is sacred.

At this point, just before the governments fall, we shall enter the second stage of my plan, the first only having prepared the ground.

Don't forget, because it's very important, that as these events unfold, you are the indisputable king of footwear. You're giving your universal sole to all citizens, from their hatching to their dispatching, if I may put it that way. Every week they replace their uppers for a few dollars, and they do it with the pleasure of being able to buy while cursing the consumer culture. And, taking advantage of this period of repudiation of governments, you won't miss the opportunity to offer shoes that express anger and rebellion. Since they're disposable, remember, your shoes can adapt daily to the moods of the people. Shoes insulting to political leaders or that show bared teeth will sell like hotcakes. Everyone will want to shout with the rest that democracy has failed. That it has reached a dead end.

Your supremacy will mean that you will be the most attentively listened to of all CEOs. Then, Mr. President, you will call a meeting of your kind to make them the proposal that they're awaiting with such impatience.

Pardon me? Fiction, you say? You credit me with a talent that I respect but do not possess, Madam. If my strategies were ludicrous, or pure creations of the imagination, I wouldn't have made a career of counselling companies but of running with those spinners of illusions we were talking about earlier. The ones who invent all those virtual worlds without which life, real life, would be so unbearable. Unbearable for people at large, who would be bored to death, and unbearable for us because people would take an interest in politics again, and would keep cramping our style.

No, Madam. I would never be dishonest enough to ask huge prices for strategies and commercial tactics based on fiction.

Your skepticism, Madam, is one of form. I mean to say, your doubts about the intelligence of my strategies are basically fuelled by your deep and growing conviction that I despise you. My conceit irritates you, and even more what you take to be a kind of misogyny on my part.

Let's deal with this sore spot before we continue. Yes, I despise you, yes, I'm conceited, and yes, I'm a misogynist. I despise you because I'm conceited. That settles two things: my conceit and the fact that I despise you. Everything's now clear on those points and nothing more needs to be said about them.

As for my misogyny, I'll give you the benefit of hearing the reason for it. Will you allow me, Mr. President? It will take a few seconds.

Thank you.

My career, Madam, has been so long and so intense that I have met hundreds, if not thousands, of people in political and economic circles. Of those hundreds, or thousands, all those whom I have judged to have the intelligence to manage our society appropriately were always … women. I surprise you, don't I? I make this confession in all sincerity but with profound disappointment. Because the whole problem arises from this: the most level-headed people of our century are women, and I am a man. That is why I am a misogynist.

The reason large corporations are evolving in such a suicidal fashion is that in the great majority they're run by men. Although men are more aggressive, they're less cunning. They're skilful over the short term, but completely outclassed when it comes to longer-term vision.

Since the early days of my career, I have helped people rise through what are called the hierarchies of power. The only ones I have ever helped have been men, even though most of the time I knew they didn't deserve the jobs I was helping them get.

Why did I help them? You don't know, obviously. Because no, you're not one of that group of women whose superiority I recognize. I'll tell you anyway why it's only the men I've always helped. It's because as long as men were running our corporations and governments, they would need me and so my career would be assured. I'm conceited, yes, conceited enough to think I'm far more effective than the vast majority of them.

Putting women behind the CEOs' desks would have made me less indispensable, since a number of them, unlike the men, would not have needed my services.

If I'm willing to admit this, Madam, it's because your President is paying me to tell him what he should do. And what I have come today to tell him to do is exactly what I have been doing myself throughout my career: place his pawns where they will be most useful to him.

In recent years, this company has grown with short-term vision. And I regret very much telling you this, Madam, but you are not the woman to have helped it see farther down the road. I despise you because, although you are a woman, you have acted like a man. There it is.

I've probably shocked you, Mr. President. I apologize. Conceit is perhaps a fault, but sincerity is not. I've been conceited since my strategies began to win, and I've been sincere since I began getting paid to produce them.

From the moment you commissioned me to put your company on the straight road, you knew my fees would give your Chief Financial Officer indigestion. That he'd have a terrible time justifying them in the quarterly report to shareholders. You called me to your rescue nevertheless because you recognized my superiority over you. So don't be offended, please, if I tell this lady, in the confines of these four walls, very sincerely what I think.

Moreover, I consider that you possess a quality that is rare and fundamental: you have a good nose. A very good nose. Though you can't see what there is, you see that there's something. Though you don't know what's going on, you know something's going on. Most of your kind neither see nor know anything. Which is why I paid you that very sincere compliment a few minutes ago.

———•———

WELL. Where were we? Ah yes. At fiction. No, Madam, what I have foreseen is not fictional. Everything will be planned as meticulously as can be, so that this company can move toward the most total and heroic achievement of its goal.

Since you've brought up the subject of fiction, and these things seem to interest you vitally, I shall take the liberty of humouring you by continuing my presentation in fictional form. Mr. President, will you allow me to take your chair? You and I will change places, if you please. I shall be you for the next few minutes. I shall be president of this company in your place.

Good. You come here. That's it. Sit in my place. Ow! No, no, it's nothing. Just my foot that … Yes. Don't mention it. Here, take my briefcase. There's nothing of consequence in it; what is important is in my head. Good.

I'm going to the other side. I'll still be facing you, but in your chair. Don't worry, I'll give it back to you soon. I've never accepted a presidency, though I've often been offered it.

There. So now I am the President. And you are the presidents of the other companies. I have called you together for this meeting we talked about, at which I will make you the proposal you've been waiting for so impatiently.

You all have in common that you run very large companies, which, like this one, as their most urgent item of business, must change the way they do things in order to ensure that they will still grow despite the alarming drop in their customers' purchasing power.

You all have in common that you have been called together just as governments are tearing their hair trying to find their way out of the hornets' nest we've got them into with our blitz of litigation of all kinds.

And you all have the immense privilege of being called together by the company that has succeeded in making disposable shoes the new norm in footgear.

So, Madam President and Messrs Presidents, I have called you together today to ask you to join with my company in the establishment of a new economic and social order. Before the close of this meeting, I will ask each of you in private whether you will follow us or not.

The decision will be yours and will be irrevocable because we have no time to lose. Those who will follow will come back for a planning session next week; those who will not I will consider consequently to have authorized me to receive their direct competitors no later than tomorrow morning. This is not a pressure tactic and I am not playing behind your backs, the proof being that I am telling you clearly now. You are entirely at liberty not to be with us and to be with the losers.

Lady and Gentlemen, our companies are sick. They have sinned by greed and now are suffering indigestion. Their growth will reach its ceiling in a few years. Those who accuse us of being on the brink of emptying the sea of its fish, emptying the Earth of its resources, and emptying the sky of its oxygen don't even care that there's worse to come: our practices are on the brink of emptying consumers of their ability to consume. Our empires are therefore at risk of collapse a few years from now. Seeing the importance of our activities in the worldwide total, this will be truly catastrophic.

In latter decades, we have directed all the resources of our intelligence, will, and imagination toward marketing anything that was marketable. We took from public authorities, which is to say, common property, all that was possible for us to appropriate and turn into private property. Together, we own and manage the better part of the primary, secondary, and tertiary activities of the majority of intelligent nations. Only nations that as yet promise no profitability, so to speak, are not totally under our control.

You know that, several months ago, our company undertook a change of direction whose effectiveness you have seen. After the implementation of a program developed at our request by one of the most brilliant strategists of our time, disposable shoes have very quickly become the standard. This program is now entering its second stage, and you are here so that you may share the benefits it will soon bring.

Before revealing the substance of this action plan that we have developed, and before specifying your role in its implementation, it is important to draw your attention to something essential to your understanding of the meticulousness with which we have constructed each of its parts.

For several months now, and you will confirm this, I'm sure, you have had no protesters underfoot. Your public relations departments have no doubt been the first to inform you of the welcome news that they no longer have to issue communiqués day after day in hope of convincing the media that you are not the monsters you were called the day before by an ecologist, or a human rights representative, or a consumer protection movement watchdog, or a rather-too-independent journalist. Why? Because the attention of agitators is all being channelled into the crisis governments are undergoing at present.

Did you know, Lady and Gentlemen, that this crisis was not brought on by a combination of circumstances or a kind of random luck, but was built from the ground up? We know because we were the ones who built it. We artificially created this untenable situation so as to obtain, with your help and co-operation, the social change that alone can save us, you and ourselves, from the business collapse we're heading for.

In a world where more and more corporations post sales figures bigger than the budgets of many States, and not among the poorest of them, it has become impossible for societies to be governed by governments. It doesn't make sense.

In a world where products and services have to sell at lower and lower prices because consumers can't afford to pay for them any more, it has become impossible for societies to function according to competitive market principles, with several companies manufacturing and selling the same product or service and being profitable. It doesn't make sense.

In a world where companies have more and more trouble maintaining their growth and increasing their profits, it has become impossible for consumers to enjoy health-care and educational services of such high quality, which cost so much and deprive us of so much money. That too doesn't make sense.

We have planned this crisis in a way that will enable us to put things right. You are here today to tell us if you wish to be among the companies that will benefit from this restructuring.

At the moment I speak, and I see you listening, populations are violently attacking their elected representatives. They accuse them of so badly managing the money they have been stealing from the people that they can no longer allocate the necessary funds for so-called public services. As you know, this complaint arises from the revelation of a great many cases of "presumed" medical error or negligence. I say "presumed" because the courts have not yet determined whether the harm done merits compensation from the ultimately responsible parties, meaning the governments. "Presumed" also because most of the cases before the courts are very questionable. A number of accusations involve events created out of thin air by lawyers who were asked to concoct truly litigious cases. To make sure the trials would be long and expensive.

The important thing, you'll agree, is for these events to monopolize the scene, fill all the newspaper pages, keep all the protesters busy. Consequently, for all the people to be expressing anger against the governments and no one else. Also, and above all, at the moment we enter the scene, for us to be heroes.

I see that you're impatient to hear this remarkable plan that I'm about to reveal. Just before coming to that, it seems to me appropriate in passing to pay tribute to the great genius of our consultant, without whom we'd be in a peck of trouble.

Forgive me, Mr. President, I was dying to play this joke for the pleasure of seeing Madam, there, boil at my monstrous conceit ... I'll continue, yes. I'll continue. I couldn't resist it...

I'll continue.

This plan does not demand that governments turn over the management of health-care services to us. It consists of doing away with them. As with education too. But not right away: progressively, almost invisibly, and so as to make people think these services are improving.

Lady and Gentlemen, in a few weeks our company will announce very officially that we will be offering free and complete health services *for life* to all who subscribe *for life* to our disposable shoes.

Here I shall pause for a few seconds to allow you to realize the sweep and reach of this move.

—•—

LISTEN carefully, please. At the foot of this building where we have our headquarters, a man is at present wearing disposable shoes that he bought this morning. He chose a pair on which we had written "Murderers" in black letters on a red ground. He chose those specifically to wear to a demonstration this afternoon outside the Department of Health office building, a regular afternoon occurrence for the past two months. When we offer him a life subscription to the disposable shoes he wears already, which, since we've given him our universal sole, will cost him $3 a pair instead of $120 a pair, when we tell him that in exchange for this subscription we're giving him free health care and education *for life*, no matter what becomes of the murderers he's denouncing, he'll sign our offer with his eyes closed. And before the ink on the contract is dry, his regard for our company will have doubled and perhaps even tripled.

I spoke of implementation in a few weeks, but the reality will be quite different. It will be more like several months because we're asking you to join our campaign so as to share both its costs and rewards, and if you join you will have to be ready. I know from experience that it will take you a certain amount of time before you're ready because your companies are very big, very cumbersome, and it's a long process for instructions to reach their destinations through those labyrinthian corridors.

We, here, have solved that problem by abolishing a great many intermediary functions to do with coordination. The coordinators were in fact only coordinating their own jobs, on orders from their unions, of course.

What will the preparation involve? What we want is for you to take our success as your model. To win absolute monopolies in your respective sectors in record time. We will help you reach that goal by teaching you how. On the other hand, you will need to perform adequately to get results, otherwise you will be replaced. I'm not talking here about replacing your company with another; I'm talking about replacing you, personally, with people trained under our supervision, whose efficacy we control.

Before moving on, I'm going to illustrate what I'm talking about with an example because I'm not at all sure you understand. You, Sir ... you're currently the leader in the very lucrative food market. You have brought your suppliers to their knees. You offer the best prices. You operate everywhere. However, you know, as I do (at least, I hope you do) that your suppliers are plotting together to replace you with a co-operative company. Right now they're passing the hat. They're preparing to challenge you with a chain of stores that will gradually nibble away your share of the market. As soon as it's in place, they'll increase the prices they charge you by ten percent to weaken you. They'll have a hard time displacing you because you're very strong and your people are pretty clever, but you probably don't much want this fight, which wouldn't help your growth, and would always carry some risk.

What you should do, Mr. President, is take our example. You should cook complete takeout meals for a price of around $1. Yes, $1. Dessert included. I'm convinced you'll manage it. You should make real treats of these meals, which will be much more economical to buy in ready-to-eat form, day after day, than buying the ingredients and preparing them oneself. This way, your stores will very quickly turn into indispensable places of food supply. Necessarily, because it will come to be considered shameful for people to spend more for the extravagant luxury of eating today what everyone else will be eating the next day anyway for a fraction of the price. A luxury that you alone, you around this table, may soon enjoy.

To succeed, you will do as we did: you will redefine the ritual of food as we redefined the symbolism of shoes. You'll invent and you'll get what you invent accepted, through price and the model to be followed. You'll replace the pleasure of cooking by the pleasure of eating like everyone else. It will be easy because cooking is a totally invented pleasure intended for those who have nothing else to do, or no other way to make themselves think they're useful somehow.

This ends my little overview of what you should do. You'll find the details in the document that I'll hand you at the end of this meeting. We have thought of everything for each one of your companies.

What you absolutely must understand from all this is that by the time all of you have changed your practices to our model, all the key sectors of the economy will be profoundly transformed, and consumers necessarily conditioned. We have blazed the trail with footwear; you will continue along the same road with food, housing, transportation, recreation, and so forth.

Understand, Lady and Gentlemen, that there's nothing new about the conditioning of consumers. We have been doing this for many years. The difference here is that we're restructuring consumption in accordance with the necessary reorientation of our activities. The consumer, far from feeling cornered, is going to be relieved. On the one hand because essential goods and services will be offered at lower prices, and on the other because he'll no longer always have to choose between fifty kinds of ice cream. For years, America has bragged of offering him all these flavours without ever considering the nightmare facing little children every time they have to turn down forty-nine of them. The golden age in marketing will not come with a multiplicity of choices, but with just one, at the best price.

Once these changes have been made in your respective industries, you'll be ready, like us, to offer life subscriptions to your products and services so that you'll be sharing the costs of health-care and educational services with us. There's no doubt at all that the vast majority of people will accept our proposals at the first opportunity. Why? Because that will be the most comfortable way to live, and also the least chancy. Once I've subscribed to the least expensive housing, the least expensive food, the least expensive clothes, and the least expensive transportation facilities, I won't have to worry about negotiating anything any more. And since my fidelity will get me free access to health care, my life will become one of extraordinary ease. Everything will be taken care of, and I'll be off the hook. We won't be far from that marvellous leisure society we've been promised for years.

I know you're impatient to learn how we've anticipated offering health-care services and reading classes without getting swallowed up in preposterous expenses. You can bet we've anticipated these things. We've anticipated never reproducing the dead ends the present governments have got themselves into.

The advantage of crisis situations like the one we've created is that they allow new models to be set up fast.

In times of relative peace, change frightens people and there are always some who take pleasure in holding it up indefinitely. Old people are specialists at this. In the twilight of their lives, they want their eyes to close finally on surroundings they know. As dilapidated as they may be. They don't want to spend that evening anywhere but in their own living rooms. If you try to change the lamp, or the armchair, or the wallpaper, they'll throw a tantrum. But they'll be the first to support change if social tensions disturb their peace.

The purpose of the discontent we stirred up was to open the way for the most far-reaching changes in the shortest time. The advent of standard meals, standard cars, standard housing would have been impossible if we hadn't first offered the model, not just of feasibility for the companies, but also mindless enthusiasm in the consumers. These things would not have been possible, either, if they had come at a time of social tranquility. Some might have accused us of manipulation or even collusion. But to the contrary, the bad guys today are the governments and only the governments, and they're so bad that all others can only be good. And if the good guys offer to take your physical well-being in hand, what reason can there be to think they could wish you ill?

The other essential point is that, to humanists, health care and education are ordinarily untouchable. Have you noticed how many people contradict themselves and become thoroughly incoherent when they call for universally dispensed health care and education for all, both in form and content? These are the same people who in ordinary times oppose any reduction in freedom of choice. Choices have to be made, that is the problem. Universality and freedom of choice are distinct and incompatible things, and the comfort of the first will always have priority over the risk associated with the second. Particularly in these times of great insecurity.

The new social contract that we will put in place, Madam President and Messrs Presidents, will give up the principle of freedom in favour of that of justice, or universality. Except for this: universality is possible only with acceptance of less quality. Health-care services will thus be universally dispensed, according to the great and fine principle of equality, only on condition of acceptance of a universal norm that will not tolerate special treatment. In other words, the people will all receive health care in the same way, that way having been defined by us, and anyone who complains about it will lose his privilege of receiving free health care. We shouldn't expect much rebellion over this because we'll be protected by our principle of universality. Protesters will quickly be branded as bumptious types trying to get special treatment.

As for health care itself, it will focus essentially on relief of pain. For several decades now, medicine has been going at things the wrong way, confusing its role with nature's. Instead of just relieving our pain, it's trying to make us immortal. If we don't rein in its research, people will soon be living to 150, even 200 years old.

This is not only against nature, it's deeply incompatible with disposable thinking. On the one hand, we have people living only for a day at a time with no thought at all for the future, and on the other, we have medicine whose aim is to prolong their lives. This is an obvious contradiction, and anyone who takes the trouble to consider it has to admit that the high priests of health care are swimming against the current in relation to the evolution of thought. Worse still, they're a social menace because they're spending our money to give us something we don't want.

The health care we will jointly offer our customers will aim not to prolong their lives but to see that they don't feel pain. People in pain consume less, are always complaining, and cost us money. Dead people consume even less, you'll tell me, but they don't cost us anything at all and don't contaminate those around them with their bellyaching. Financially speaking, it's vastly preferable to see them die younger and in less pain.

As regards education, which we will also offer free of charge, I shall limit my remarks to a few words.

The natural evolution of our society will lead gradually to the disappearance of schools. Our commitment to educate our customers free of charge will very soon be no more than theoretical, and I predict that it will be the people themselves who will downgrade the needs in the sector, contrary to the case in health care.

Culture, Lady and Gentlemen, is an accident of History. Education has made the same mistake as health care; it has aimed to educate beyond needs and in flagrant contradiction of the trend today as defined by disposable thought. In almost all sectors, we have made the mistake of educating people well beyond our needs, and theirs. To such a point that we have produced people who think too much and derive only doubts and discomfort from their education. It has been proven that less educated people ask less questions of themselves and are generally happier. It has also been proven that those who get in our way most often are those who have spent most time at school desks and today spend more time in an office looking for something to do than in a factory producing something useful.

Education will soon be limited to learning the strict necessities: reading, counting, controlling a machine that has to be run. I didn't say *understanding*; I said *learning*. The difference is colossal because the minute you begin to understand, you inevitably begin to ask questions.

And since our society is going to be providing less and less answers, it would be wise not to invite questions.

The problem with culture is that it doesn't produce anything. We tolerated the existence of this luxury a few centuries ago because its means of diffusion were hardly developed at all and its reach was therefore limited. Today, however, culture has the capacity to contaminate our people. A very theoretical capacity, fortunately, because we lost no time taking over the tools of diffusion so they would leave as little room as possible for perverted content. But we cannot be too careful and our investments in education will be planned with infinite care to conform with disposable thought. This will surely please our customers, who will be relieved not to have to read Shakespeare, or waste their time learning who Robespierre was, or what an ecosystem is, or where the Philippines are. The arts will be replaced by the art of living, and the few rebels who express their disgruntlement in verse will find themselves in the place they occupied in Antiquity, the one reserved for visionaries, itinerant clowns who were better at raising laughs than rousing rabbles.

What will happen to governments, you're saying? I'm surprised you didn't ask me this question earlier. Allow me to reply with this question: why do we need governments at all? Government too is a very recent, very human invention. Even its existence is contrary to the teachings of nature. Doesn't the expression, *human nature*, spell out that nature is not *a priori* human, and that we humans are denaturing it?

You all know the law of nature. It's the only law applied without being promulgated or enforced by any government. Our initiative will be the most natural possible: it will obey only this law, the law of the jungle, by which the strongest wins. At this time, we are the strongest. It will be natural therefore that the law will be laid down by us.

Please take note that we will assuredly be more efficient than any of the governments our society has had to endure in recent centuries. We make a great deal of the freedom and justice characteristic of our so-called advanced society. We trumpet our social achievements, the result of our advanced sense of societal organization. But I challenge you to find a single individual who doesn't feel a prisoner of his advanced society.

Our intervention will be applauded as a necessary move. When we redefine behaviour patterns with regard to consumption, we will liberate people from the market mentality that hems them in and poisons their existence. We are going to transform the consumer into a human being through the simple act of freeing him of the obligation to be a consumer. Which at the same time will be our ultimate achievement as companies because we will have made a new man exquisitely moulded to our needs for our growth.

Pardon me? Yes, Sir, I know perfectly well what I'm saying. This strategy, which you will follow along with the rest of us because you have no other choice, will see the disappearance of consumption such as you and I have known it to date, and will bring forth a new man.

But let's take back our own places now, Mr. President. For the conclusion of my presentation, I'd rather be myself again.

There. Thank you. Your chair is certainly comfortable, but I always like getting back to my own. At my age, there's nothing like being in one's cozy old slippers.

———

WHAT I wanted to say is that from the moment we are the ones who decide what the consumer consumes, and at the same time are taking over from governments the role they have assigned themselves and are no longer capable of assuming, strictly speaking our activities will no longer be commercial, and strictly speaking man will no longer be a consumer. Consumption having been increasingly dragged through the mud, you'll agree that this is excellent news.

If there's going to be consumption, there have to be consumers, Lady and Gentlemen. But those consumers are not going to exist any more, in a sense; at least, soon they'll no longer have any choices to make. Once you've become the only company making shoes, and everyone is a life subscriber to your products, it goes without saying that you'll no longer have any reason to keep making a wide variety of models. People will wear the ones you make. Without fuss, and happy to be taken care of.

Will you complain about it? Surely not. Isn't this what you've been after since you were first in business? Why would you want to keep growing and growing some more if not to become the new Caesars holding sway over your empire? It certainly isn't to boost your profits, because a large piece of the planet is already yours.

On my island in Greece, a number of peasants make a living picking olives that they never suspect will end up a few months later in the martini glass of a scientist who's researching our genetic code. These peasants don't even know what a gene is, though they have a genius of their own. From this I've learned something: that there's no connection between olives and genes. And every time a connection is found, it's because we've made up our minds about it. Yes, made up our minds. Unscrupulously.

Mr. President, you will decide, no later than tomorrow, to put this plan into operation. I'm so convinced of it that I'm leaving tomorrow for that island where only one thing remains for me to do before I disappear forever, and that's to write the final chapter of the history of man.

This chapter will be very short because once this strategy I have just presented is in place, the history of man will cease to evolve forevermore. It will set like the history of plants, and will undergo only what might be called climatic changes.

Why, you ask me? Because, Sir, man exists and evolves only to the extent that he consumes. If I were not convinced of it, not absolutely certain, I would never have made my career in this field. I might have gone on the stage. They say I have some talent for that, too.

Mr. President, you'll no doubt be very proud to hear that the heroine of this chapter I'm preparing to write will be your daughter. She's the very portrait of what the human race of tomorrow will be. People of no ambition who are comfortably settled in inertia and whose notion of the future has been supplanted by an eternal present. Will they make music together? Yes, probably. Might as well while away the time.

Oh! I see it's nearly three o'clock already. This meeting has taken more time than expected. I hope I haven't bored you. I've often been chided for talking too much. Fortunately, I've never been chided for having nothing to say.

Since my plane is at four o'clock, I'll leave you my bill, go downstairs, and jump in a taxi. I won't wait for your cheque. I trust you.

Lady and Gentlemen, I'll leave you now. I'll even bid you adieu because we won't see each other again. I've done what I came to do. I've done as I was asked, and now I'm signing off.

Good day to you.

Ah, my briefcase! Thank you. I would have forgotten it. There are no papers in it, no. Only a parachute. Yes, a parachute. That's odd, you'll tell me, but I detest aeroplanes. Heights give me vertigo.

ABOUT THE AUTHOR

SINCLAIR DUMONTAIS is the pseudonym of a writer who works in marketing and communications. He is the founder of and a contributor to Dialogus (WWW.DIALOGUS2.ORG), an interactive website that allows for discourse on social, political, and philosophical issues. He has also published four other books, including his first novel, *L'Empêcheur.* He lives in Quebec City, Quebec.

ABOUT THE TRANSLATOR

PATRICIA CLAXTON is the Governor General's Award-winning translator of *Enchantment and Sorrow* by Gabrielle Roy and *Gabrielle Roy: A Life* by François Ricard, which also won the Drainie–Taylor Biography Prize. She has also received four other Governor General's Award nominations and three Canada Council Honourable Mentions for Translation. Her most recent translation, *A Sunday at the Pool in Kigali* by Gil Courtemanche, was shortlisted for the Governor General's Award and the Rogers Writer's Trust Fiction Prize. She lives in Montreal, Quebec.